Kizzy Ann Stamps

W9-CFC-197

Kizzy Ann Stamps

JERI WATTS

SCHOLASTIC INC.

This is a work of fiction. Names, characters, places, and incidents are either
products of the author's imagination or, if real, are used fictitiously.

No part of this publication may be reproduced, stored in a retrieval
system, or transmitted in any form or by any means, electronic, mechanical,
photocopying, recording, or otherwise, without written permission of the publisher.
For information regarding permission, write to Candlewick Press,
99 Dover Street, Somerville, MA 02144.

ISBN 978-0-545-61478-8

Copyright © 2012 by Jeri Watts.
All rights reserved. Published by Scholastic Inc.,
557 Broadway, New York, NY 10012,
by arrangement with Candlewick Press.
SCHOLASTIC and associated logos are trademarks
and/or registered trademarks of Scholastic Inc.

12 11 10 9 8   16 17 18/0

Printed in the U.S.A.   40

First Scholastic printing, September 2013

This book was typeset in Scala.

To Chuck, Chandler, and Mary Carson,
who have been with me for every up and down
of the writing life. Thank you for making
this book possible.

July 1, 1963

Dear Miss Anderson,

My teacher, Mrs. Warren, says I have to write you, and when Mrs. Warren says to do something, you do it. She has taught at the black school for thirty-seven years. My daddy does what she says, the preacher does what she says, and you'd better believe I do what she says. And she said that in the spirit of working together, all us black kids should write you letters over the summer so you can get to know us a bit before we start at the white school in September.

So, here I am, writing to you.

I never thought I'd write to the teacher at the white school. I don't know as I've ever thought about the white school, really, before all this integration business got started. But here I am, fixing to go there come September.

I guess I should introduce myself. My name is Kizzy Ann Stamps. I like reading most everything, but I hate history. I just don't really care what some dead folks did or said two hundred years ago.

Sorry, guess that isn't trying to work together, the way Mrs. Warren wants. But Mrs. Warren would tell you I'm trouble in her class, and I guess that's fair. I say what I think quite often—too often, she says—and I ask questions. Lots of questions. And I don't like to be bossed. Stand up for something, that's what I say.

So I'm going to stand up now and tell you the truth, even if it means you won't like me. (My brother says you won't like any of the black kids. You just have to accept us.) But I believe in telling the truth. So here it is: I don't want to change to a white school. Just so you know. I don't want to.

I guess I should say the integrated school. My folks

are all aflutter about it, and Mrs. Warren says this is an
"opportunity." When she says it, the word is in capital
letters and lit up like the beer sign down at Shorty's
Pool Hall. Even though it means she is out of a job and
we will all have to walk farther to school.

So I don't want to come. Now you know.

July 3, 1963

Well, I thank you for writing back, Miss. You could have
knocked me down with a feather when the mailman
said he had a letter for me. He put it in my hand special like. My whole family was in awe of me getting a
letter addressed to me *alone,* with that fancy script writing on the outside, my name looking like a machine
wrote it in that practically perfect writing of yours!
That envelope and the writing paper are so creamy
and thick. . . . I haven't ever held on to paper like that
before. Mrs. Warren gave us paper to write our letters
to you. I go to her house each time I need new paper
and she gives me more. She told me she will give me
as much as I want, but paper is not something we just

have lots of sitting around. I didn't even know it came in different *types*. I guess there are lots of things I don't know, though.

For example, I don't know as I ever expected that you really would *read* my letter—never mind asking me questions about myself. You said you wanted to know more about how I make trouble for Mrs. Warren, and I can give you a perfect example. We can go along, she and I, and I'll think we're right like two peas in a pod, and then I find out I just can't go along with her way of thinking at all. Like she is always saying education is important, and it isn't that I disagree with that—no, ma'am. I know education is important. Mrs. Warren says equal education is the "way out of poverty" and the "answer to prejudice." So writing well and reading well are crucial. I don't disagree with that. I read and write well. I've worked hard to learn those things—sometimes I trip up and say "ain't," but I really see what Mrs. Warren says about how sounding educated is the language of money, the language of getting ahead. Still, Mrs. Warren won't bend at all. For instance, she only considers you a good writer if you stick with *her* topics. Topics like heroes and good solid role models, such as Frederick Douglass, George Washington Carver, and Rosa Parks. Not a dog.

See, she told us to write about who we most admire. Most of the kids wrote about grandmothers or mothers, uncles or dads. Brenda Stevens wrote about Rosa Parks (and Brenda Stevens doesn't even like Rosa Parks, because she had to sit in church an extra hour one time listening to a lady who had met her), and Chester Whitehouse wrote six pages on Dr. Martin Luther King Jr. Everybody knows Mrs. Warren thinks the sun rises and sets with Dr. King. She read his "Letter from Birmingham Jail" three times to us in one week, and then she said, "His voice rings out in my ears, in my soul, and in the future of this nation." It's no wonder Chester was teacher's pet for a flat-out month. I didn't write about any of those folks, though. I wrote about Shag.

Shag is white and black, like all border collies. She has weepy eyes. I wonder sometimes if she's sad, but I think she doesn't cry so much as her eyes just leak a little. Anyway, I hope so.

I've done some checking on border collies, because my daddy didn't really know what kind of dog Shag was when we found her wandering near our back ten acres. I went to the library Miss Anne Spencer has, for black folks, and looked in the *Encyclopedia Britannica*, which has just about everything you would ever want to know. I was looking at pictures and trying to figure out about Shag, but Miss Anne Spencer knows a lot (she is a real poet, after all, got her stuff in books, you know—and she's a librarian to boot), so when I described Shag, she said, "A border collie, most likely," and snap, there you have it. She flipped to border collies, and sure enough, she was right. I discovered border collies are a registered breed in Scotland. People have been bringing them to the United States for a while, but not much at all in these parts. I have the only one around here, far as I know.

I feed her every day—Shag likes her scraps—but the most important thing for Shag is to work. That's the way border collies are. She brings in the cattle for milking every day, crouching low and nipping at their heels. I think if she didn't get to do this, she really *would* cry.

As a breed, border collies are pigheaded, and I'm guessing that's why Shag was wandering. Lots of folks dump their dogs in the country, and I reckon Shag wasn't good at doing what she didn't want, so she got dumped.

Daddy says she is a working dog and as long as she's working, she's happy and obeys. She *will* obey me, no matter what, so that's why my daddy says she's mine. The only thing she doesn't obey me on is sleeping in my room—I've always wanted a dog who will sleep on the hook rug next to my bed. As I tucked in on those first nights, I'd tell her, "Stay." But night after night, she'd go out and sleep beside our mule, Zero. After I fell asleep, she'd slip out of my room and go to the front door and stand there staring with her deep chocolate eyes until one of my parents would let her out. My daddy finally said, "Kizzy Ann, face it. She's just not comfortable in the house. She's a working dog, not a house pet." But she is mine, and except for that one thing, she always obeys me, always.

So, anyway, she is a hard worker on a farm that needs hard work, and a survivor, since she made it on her own after she got dumped by whoever owned her, and I wrote in my assignment that she is the being I most admire. Mrs. Warren didn't even put a grade on my paper. She gave it back and said, "You can't write about any dog."

I said, "You said to write about who we most admire. And to me, that's Shag."

That led to my final switching of the year. Mrs. Warren told me to rewrite my paper about a person, but I stuck to my guns and turned the same paper in again. So, on the last day of school, when Mrs. Warren told us that we were all going to read our last writing assignment for the class, she made it clear I wouldn't be reading. "We shall all read the delightful pieces on the person we admire most. All, that is, except for Kizzy Ann. Now, my dear, there is no sense looking askance. You knew I wanted you to rewrite it, but you remained stubborn."

I couldn't help it—the words just popped out of me when she called me stubborn. "That's not fair," I said. "I wrote exactly what I felt, and that should count for something. It's the truth, and I shouldn't have to change the truth."

The hush that spread was thick as my granny's apple butter heaped on a biscuit. And the look from

Mrs. Warren was one that scraped that hush down to an unnatural quiet.

"A switch, if you please," she said. When Mrs. Warren gets all ladylike in her speech, you know things are bad.

Still, I tell you I didn't feel the switch that day. Because I knew I was right.

And you know what? There's another particular thing I admire about Shag that I didn't even put in the paper. Shag is the only one in the world who doesn't sneak glances at my scar. She just looks me in the eye, dead on, and I prefer that. You'd think I was a monster, the way people slide their glances around at me.

I know I haven't told you about my scar yet. So here goes: Three years ago, when I was nine, I was helping at the Feaganses'. You may not be a farm girl, so maybe you don't know how at harvesttime everybody helps. Everybody. So don't go thinking my parents were bad or nothing, letting a nine-year-old help. I've helped with chores since I was way little.

I was working next to Frank Charles Feagans — it

was his family's farm—and we were using the scythes to cut some of the old cornstalks. (Mr. Feagans is a finicky farmer, not liking to just turn his cows loose in the field to take care of the cornstalks with their steady munching. I think it's because he's white—hope that doesn't offend you.) Anyway, Frank Charles couldn't stop looking at Shag—she'd just come to us—and he turned fast, following Shag with his eyes. He knocked against me and set me off balance. I put my hands out and fell.

Right into the sweep of Frank Charles's scythe.

The cut went from the tip of my right eye to the corner of my smile, and I know I looked a sight, because when my daddy pulled me up, he had turned ashy. Frank Charles fainted on the spot, and Shag started barking at everybody. Daddy says she was trying to get us to help me. I remember being carried faster than I'd ever believed Daddy could go across a field of broken cornstalks—we flew. I know Shag was beside us, because I had no control over my hands— they were hanging limp by my daddy's legs—and I could feel Shag's delicate lick against my flesh every now and again. Step, step, step, lick, step, step, step, lick. I suppose it hypnotized me a bit, because I really don't remember anything else till I woke up in my bed with old Doc Morris peering into my face.

He slid a finger next to my cheek, and I heard Shag growling. "Ain't hurting her," Doc Morris murmured. "Just looking for reflexes, pup." I heard Shag settle beside my bed, and when they all left, Mama and Daddy patting my feet and trying not to cry, I felt Shag jump up and lie down beside me. I went to sleep with my fingers curled tight in her fur.

July 5, 1963

Mama says it is bad manners to stop in the middle of a story, so if she knew that last letter I sent you ended like that, in the middle, she'd probably make me get a switch, but I'm not really sorry. I think the best stories are the ones that build suspense and make you wonder what happened next.

Did you wonder what happened to me next?

When I woke up, it was just getting light. I lay there, thinking back to the day before, and I was afraid to touch my cheek. But the Good Lord says you got to meet your problems head-on, so I eased up out of my bed and walked on shaky legs to the sliver of looking glass we have in the hall. (My granny says it is pure vanity what makes my mama hang up a piece of mirror to look on herself, but Mama still hung it up and looks on it every day.)

I turned my head back and forth and saw a huge bandage covering my cheek. There was dried blood in my hair, and the edges of the bandage were dark and stained. I was surprised because I didn't feel a thing. I realized I felt nothing because of the painkiller. The whole side of my head had a heavy, weighted feeling. I got back in the bed and felt myself starting to shake all over.

Before you could say "jackrabbit," Shag was coming back in, her toenails clicking across the floor. She eased up next to me, her warm, grassy breath surrounding me, her body pressing mine until I stopped my desperate shaking and fell back into dozing.

She was like that, by my side, for weeks as I healed, as my skin knit together and I came to terms with my future. She never slept in the room, but she was there most of every day. It was a sacrifice for Shag, I know, because working the farm is what she enjoys, but she stayed with me. I'd wake up to see her looking out the window, listening to the bellowing of the cows, and it was like her whole body was aching to go to them, yet she did not go. She'd turn her head back and lick my face, not quite touching the bandages, knowing that wasn't allowed, but telling us both she was tending me, she was working here, working me instead of the farm animals. Little by little, she made me leave my bed, herded me out of my blankets, forced me out of my carved-out pillow space. When friends or gawkers came by, she nestled over against the wall where I liked to rest my injured cheek and pushed me to face them, to look at them head-on, to get the stares over and done with, but always with her to lean on, always with her support.

Mama says it was the most important work that dog has ever done.

Daddy says, "That there is some kind of dog."

He's got that right.

One time, during my healing, I watched outside my

window when my brother, James, and his best friend, Cabbie Simpson, went through a ritual to become blood brothers, pricking their fingers and mixing their blood up. I thought I might do the same with Shag. Then she would have a scar, too, and she would be my sister. I called her to my bed, and she came, edging up beside me. She put her paw in my lap, as I asked her to, and I rubbed it, smoothed it.

She began to gently lick my scar for me, because by then it had scarred up. I think she sensed that we were . . . what? Exchanging in some way? Looking out for each other? She began to sniff my scar, too, sniff my hairline, then lay down and fell asleep. Shag goes through her life depending on her sense of smell, you know. Dogs have to. So even though I *thought* I was thinking about cutting us, she knew I really wasn't. Because she smelled that she could trust me. She knows the smell of trust.

So we're not sisters by blood after all. We're just us.

I have to say one more thing before Daddy takes this to the mailbox. I cannot believe I am writing all of this to you. And more amazing, I cannot really believe you are reading it and writing back. It is stranger to me than Santa Claus or the Tooth Fairy used to be. . . . It just feels so good to say some things I've been wanting to say for so long, things I didn't even really know wanted saying.

July 6, 1963

Miss Anderson, I am so sorry you've never had a dog. What a disappointment for you that your father had allergies. If you would like, sometime, you can meet my Shag, if you want to. It isn't the same as having your own, of course. I'm glad you had Mr. Boxster, even though turtles aren't as good as dogs. James had a turtle once, but I dropped him and he died. I didn't mean to, but when I picked him up, he kept moving his legs, and it felt so nasty, the way his legs felt against my fingers, I let go, and even though I was only three, he fell from my eyeball height to the floor. That isn't any small-potatoes height when you are a turtle, I guess. I suppose his little innards couldn't take the drop. We buried him.

So now you won't be surprised when you meet

me. I've told you just about everything there is to tell, I think. My scar is sizable, I suppose. People do stare. And it aches plenty when the weather socks in. Mama calls me Moon Child, because the scar is shaped like a crescent moon. Sometimes, when people hear Mama call me that, they look askance, like they think that is horrible, but I think it is special. It seems like a bond between us, somehow, that she turned what many people think of as my tragedy into a special name between us.

I admit, though, I don't like it when folks stare. Most of the folks around here know me and have seen that scar, so you'd think that would just be that, but scars on your face seem to be hard to turn away from. I feel hot when they're staring, and I can't keep my eyes from turning down to the ground. I get mad at myself for looking down. What do I have to look down about? Why do I have to feel ashamed? I was doing honest work. It wasn't my fault that Frank Charles hit my arm. It wasn't my fault I was being neighborly to a family that doesn't even help mine—that old Mr. Feagans is too mean to help black people but takes help from anybody when his crops need pulling in! It wasn't my fault.

What will probably be harder for you to turn away from more than my scar is the attitude I have, the one that Mrs. Warren says needs "serious adjustment." She has been my one and only teacher so far, but I figure you will find me as trying as she does.

When I came to our schoolhouse, I was six years old and tiny. Mrs. Warren explained to us that in your school you have actual classrooms for different grades. We just have the one room, so everybody is in the same room. Mrs. Warren put me in the front row—where everybody starts—and then you move back by rows depending on how smart you show yourself to be, by how much you know. So you can have older kids sitting in the front row with the littlest kids—it doesn't matter. It took me only half a day to get my rightful place two rows back, even if I was just six years old. I knew letters and numbers (I read everything I can get my hands on), and I could add, subtract, and read whole parts of the Bible, including several psalms. (I can do *all* the psalms now, but some of those words are killers when you've just started reading. King David knew some powerful complicated words. I admit that the Bible is pretty much the only book at my house because of Granny Bits, and there's lots of times when I'm bitten by the reading bug, so you see why I could already read whole parts of the Bible when I started school.)

'Course, it wasn't but an hour into the day when I was sent out to get my first switch. I'd done what Mrs. Warren would not allow—I'd interrupted her and asked "Why?"

Even back then at six, I could tell that a part of Mrs. Warren was downright excited to have a student ask anything. But she had forty-two students on days when everybody came, and she would have *order* in her classroom, let me tell you. So you didn't interrupt, and if you had questions you had two options—write them for her to answer later or look it up yourself. But she really wanted you to do it yourself. I do look things up—I really like to find out stuff for myself—but there are times I don't want to wait. I want to know NOW!

We didn't have reference books in our classroom.

Do you have reference books in your room? Maybe even encyclopedias? I love encyclopedias—you can learn all manner of stuff collected right in one place! That could be one good thing about integrated schools, if I could see and use some reference books in class.

For now I go to Miss Anne Spencer's library near downtown Lynchburg. I know I told you she was a poet. She must love words aplenty—writing them, reading them, and surrounding herself with them in every way. Only white folks can use the city library—well, of course you know that, but it bears saying because what I am going to say next is so amazing. Miss Anne (we call her Miss Anne as a sign of respect, even though she is married and has children) has been inside of the white library once—I don't know if she was allowed in somehow or she just sneaked—and she says it is a building full of light, books, and knowing.

Her family's house, which is where our library is located, is dark in the rooms where she keeps the books, so they'll stay in good shape for longer. She has her life going on in that house amid the books. It's a busy place, a tumble of life and knowledge, fun and facts. So it may not be light, but it is a place of books and knowing.

I'd like the light, though.

July 6, 1963 — continued

I have a lot to tell you, so I went and got more paper! (By the way, I like how our letters are crossing each other in the mail—this way it isn't just straight answering each other's questions—we had pen pals once, from a class all the way over in Campbell County, and my pen pal had about as much imagination as could be in Shag's toenail! All she could do was answer a question, then ask the same question back at me. It was like talking to a wall. This way is much better. I never know what you will say to me, and I'm betting you likely never know what I will say to you.)

Today Shag and I went into the woods to round up kindling. It's a job that needs doing every so often, and it was a good way to get out of helping with the garden, which is flat-out hot this time of year.

Shag likes work such as this. She herds me toward

big piles of sticks, which makes my time more useful. I create big, big piles and then guide my brother to them with his wheelbarrow. He'll gather them, pile by pile, and we'll have kindling for the winter.

I had a substantial pile building—and Shag was all over the place, bouncing here and there, yapping to me when she saw good kindling—when I saw that Frank Charles Feagans coming. I already mentioned him, and I bet you know him, being as he is white and you teach at the white school.

I don't know if you say bad things about your students or not, but I have to tell the truth. Frank Charles is just a pain in my side. (He might even be a teacher's pet, like a couple of people I have already mentioned in here, but I wouldn't know, since I haven't been in class with him. I wouldn't put it past him, though.) He lives on the next farm over, and even though we have farmed our place for nigh onto three generations (my ancestors got it fair and square after the war), Mr. Feagans doesn't take kindly to having darkies (that's what he calls us, and I really hate that word) living so close. He even moved his home-place across his land and built a whole new house so as not to have to see our land when he gets up of a morning. I wonder how Frank Charles feels, seeing cows in his old living room and hay stored up tighter than a tick on a dog's head in the whole upstairs of his childhood.

I'll admit I'm still holding it against Frank Charles that he was a part of me getting this scar. I don't care so much about being pretty—I'm not one of those prissy girls, you know—but who would want to be stared at all of life instead of being able to blend in when it's useful? I can't ever blend in.

I saw him and all my bad feelings started boiling under my skin, so I turned my back to him and pretended I didn't see him. Granny Bits says this is a message, body language, but apparently it is a foreign language to Frank Charles. He just kept on coming, calling out as he closed in. "My daddy says you aren't supposed to be stealing our kindling. These woods are Feagans land."

"Your daddy is a liar and you know it, Frank Charles Feagans. You've got a fence you climbed to get here, and that borders your farm plain as day."

"He's gonna be mad when he finds out."

showing some tooth. She snarled low and sank on her front legs, a pre-attack look for sure.

Mr. Feagans and Frank Charles backed up a bit. "Yeah," Mr. Feagans said. "Yeah, he does, but paper can lie just like any darky."

I let him get that last word, because I could tell he wasn't going to take any chances with Shag around. Still, I didn't linger. I know at least as much as our dumbest milk cow. Where's there barking, sooner or later, there'll be a bite.

July 10, 1963

Oh, my gosh! Thank you so much for the creamy paper you sent for me to write you on! Holding it's like being rich! I don't know that I really want to write on it, but I know that is what it's for, so I am doing it right now. I didn't show anyone but my family this gift. It seemed too special, too incredible that you would do this. Mama says you are not to send me stationery like this anymore, but thank you for doing it this one time, because I feel like I am a fairy-tale princess or something.

I thank you kindly for writing back to me again. And letters to all the students! It is all over the community, how all of us got those creamy letters. Mrs. Warren is walking around like she made the world move—your letter to her was the topper, and she has shown it to everybody, and she told the preacher he would need to have parts of it in his sermon on Sunday. Granny Bits is filling our house with all sorts of bad talk about how pride goes before a fall, but Daddy says never mind, Mrs. Warren deserves a good chance to show off, since she is working hard for the children of the community and she gave up her job to help it happen. (I didn't think much about how Mrs. Warren had to give up her job—since she's as old as Methuselah, I just thought she might *want* to stop working. She *ought* to want to stop working.) I got to say, that did make Granny Bits hush in a hurry.

I know how the others are feeling. Before you wrote, I'd never had a letter from a teacher before. It's a little like getting a letter from God! Don't tell Granny Bits I said that, though—I'm pretty sure I'd get a switching for that! Those must be some great schools, that teach all the teachers. Y'all's handwriting looks exactly the same, you and Mrs. Warren's, and I admit, it is always easy to read, not like my scribble-scrabble. It's almost like a handwriting machine, churning out same-shaped letters and numbers. I've watched Mrs. Warren write on our papers before, and she is as precise as any farm machinery we own, all sharp and sure, taking the time to touch lines and form those loops. I don't think I'll ever have that kind of patience, but it sure is like watching an artist at work. Did it take you hours to write all those letters?

Did you write letters of welcome to your white kids, too? I guess you have to, to make things fair, but I hope you didn't. They are always welcome. We're the ones trying something new, being made to go where we aren't wanted and aren't really wanting to go. But maybe I don't really want you to answer the question, so don't tell me, okay? I'm just going to pretend you wrote to only us. I know that's kind of being a baby, but I think this one time I want to believe you'd treat us more special than the others.

It's very interesting to hear more about you. I realize you've mostly just written to me about me in your other letters. I guess I thought you'd have come from far away, not grown up right over in Lynchburg. Still, I don't think your world has been exactly like mine. I won't hold that against you, though. I hope you won't hold it against me.

Sure, I could tell you about our farm, since you asked. I tend to skip describing things sometimes—when I read a story, once I know where it happens, snap, I can figure out what it looks like and I don't need the author to go on for four pages with all that flowery description, you know what I mean? But Mrs. Warren says some readers like to be "grounded in the place," and I suppose you could be one of those readers. So, our farm has a smallish farmhouse built by Stamps folks over the years. The earliest part was just one room, built by the Stamps who got the land when they scraped together some money after they were slaves. That room is now the kitchen (they used it for everything back then, according to Granny Bits). The ceiling in there hangs low—my daddy is about six feet tall and he kind of stoops in there, but in a friendly way. The walls are a soft yellow, and it is my favorite room because it is always warm and it smells like toast and tomatoes even when nothing is cooking. Granny Bits spends lots of her time there, when she cooks and when she irons. We often seem to gather there to tell each other about our day after things have happened. We often go there to get a little silly talk. It's where we play board games and where I usually get my homework done, since I don't have a fancy desk in my room. The other rooms in the house sort of got added on as needed, so the house feels like a quilt to me. I don't know if that makes sense, but that's how it seems to me, like a quilt with pieces all patched together, fitted just so.

Our land is spread around twenty acres, and we have some crops, a garden, and some milk cows, a few pigs, chickens, a rooster, and one meat cow, sometimes two in a good year. I help with the crops, the garden, and the milking. The chickens and some of the cooking are my jobs too. Mama and Daddy respect that I don't want to help much with the pigs and meat cows—I don't want to get on a first-name basis with something I might have to eat later on. And of course, the rooster is ornery, so I avoid him all the time.

Phew! Is that enough describing?

Did you like football when you went to high school? I don't care, particularly, but my brother, James, plays football at the high school. Well, that isn't really the truth. He's still practicing at the black school field. Football doesn't seem to have gotten integrated like the school. The coach said there isn't room at the high-school field for everybody, and he says none of the black boys are ready for the varsity squad because they haven't faced the right kind of competition. So all the black players are on the junior varsity team, and it practices over at the old school. James says it is fine by him, 'cause it feels like normal. But I think he must be angry about it, because he's a senior, and his dream since he was very little was to be the star of the home-coming game, and even though the coach says JV will have a homecoming game too, it isn't *the* game.

Talking about this makes me feel right nervous about starting at your school, Miss. Plus, to be honest, I just don't know if I'll be able to work with all those white kids around. My mama says this is a chance for me to prove to Frank Charles and others that I'm just as good as they are.

I'll tell you a secret: I sure hope they'll see that I am.

July 25, 1963

I'm anxious to see your school building, Miss Anderson. Our building is squat and square, slatted on the sides with planed boards the newly freed slaves slapped together in their excitement for a school the first time it was legal for my people to learn. While it is true that they put it together in a flurry, they tried to do it with some care because the school was an important place. It was important to my family, for sure, because some of my ancestors had already had some learning. Like Granny Bits told me about Rainser. He is one of my ancestors who'd had to learn in secret. He worked in the fields during the day, but at night, all secret like, he learned to spell and write his name. I don't think he learned much else, but he learned that. I don't know who taught him either, but it was dangerous for both of them, that's for sure. There were others in the family—Granny Bits has a list of them, and I had to memorize them for her back when I was seven, to prove I appreciated my heritage and had respect for schooling. It was interesting to me anyway, I'll tell you, but I do like choosing what I do outside of school, so it did rankle me, I admit, when she *made* me do it. Of course, I know better than to question Granny Bits— last time I did that, I couldn't sit down comfortably for three days, so I kept that rankle to myself!

Anyway, you can see why the school was and is so important to my people. Granny Bits says this building was put up before some folks had their own homes. We've used the same building ever since. It doesn't have a floor to speak of, just swept dirt. Mr. Felix, our custodian, who I swear is two hundred years old, is supposed to keep the place clean and tidy. He comes in every day. He's bald-headed and shrinking away as he ages, his eyes getting more and more stuck out with every year, and he looks around the room like it has gotten bigger every day. His head sticks out of his shirt like an old turtle—you know, those old tortoises that are hundreds of years old? He pokes his head into this corner and that corner and says, "Looks pert clean to me, no cobbsywebs here, no cobbsywebs there."

What he knows is that Mrs. Warren cannot abide dirt of any kind, and she will get so fed up with the dirt and the cobwebs that she will get out that broom and clean it herself every day and then he won't have to do it! Then off he goes, to wherever he hides, to smoke or whatever, his old eyes smiling because he has tricked her again. That old dirt floor gets cold come winter, but we all bring wood for the chimney, and Mrs. Warren can build a mean fire, let me tell you. She lays that kindling in first thing of a morning and keeps the fire stoked so that it never dies out. The earliest learners get a bit hot, as they sit closest to the fire, and the high-schoolers are farthest out, so they can get a mite cold, but those of us who sit middlin' are nice and toasty. I guess I'm lucky I haven't learned all there is to learn just yet!

We had a heater donated two years ago by Ganell Woodruff, the biggest success story around here, who invented something I don't understand but lives in Detroit and writes letters to Mrs. Warren regularly, telling her how great he is. This time, instead of a letter, he put his money where his mouth is and actually sent a heater. It had instructions, and Mr. Felix was going to hook it up. He started on a Saturday, but it took him forever and he was still finishing up on Monday morning. It clung to the low ceiling like a weighty beetle, which is not what any of us expected. Mrs. Warren would not let us sit at our desks, made us all stand behind her like little chickens behind the hen when Mr. Felix went to light it, him perched on this little three-rung ladder while she stood nearby and we peered around her, anxious to feel the heat pulsing out of the great warming box.

"Do you have any idea what you are doing, Felix?"

"Reckon I do, ma'am," he answered.

"Then light the contraption," she commanded.

He lit it.

It blew up.

Well, not completely. But it sparked and went *boom*. Mr. Felix jumped off that ladder like he was a spry sixteen, his legs filled with energy he probably never knew he had. Mrs. Warren spread her arms to shield us, her protective instincts mother-henning us, and we, the little chickens, herded behind her and ridiculously tried to fit behind her huge bottom. What a sight we must have been. The heater slowly, sadly sagged, then belched, then plopped onto the dirt floor.

"You all right, Mr. Felix?" Mrs. Warren asked.

Mr. Felix had his eyelashes, eyebrows, and what little hair had been on the front of his head singed right off. But he'd squeezed his eyes closed, and so, yes, besides having the bejeebers scared out of him and losing all his hair, he was all right. Mrs. Warren gave him the rest of the day off, telling him we'd "work around that monster for the rest of the day." I heard she got her husband to come up that evening and heave it off to the junkyard. Next day, we just all brought wood again, and that was the end of the hanging heater.

I hope you don't have a heater hanging from your ceiling!

I know I shouldn't do this, but I'll go ahead because you know I talk about everything. . . . Bathrooms. We have an outhouse—we have to go outside. I'm guessing you don't, but that's where the problem comes in, because James says we're not going to get to use the bathroom with the white kids. I know I can't ever use the ones in town, no matter how bad I have to go. I've just got to hold it or find a place in the woods. Am I going to have to hold it all day?

I hope you don't mind if I write you about something different from school. I didn't want to end my letter on that question of the bathroom—that seemed just too awful, you know? So, I thought I'd talk about what we do for fun. We go to baseball games. We don't go to the Lynchburg games. That's a long way into town, for one thing, and it is kind of awkward anyhow, with James. He gets all mad, because there's nothing but white players on the Lynchburg team. Since Jackie Robinson integrated major-league baseball, you'd think minor-league teams like Lynchburg would be mixed, and they *can* be, but they're often not, and it drives James crazy. So, he's no fun for any of us to be around, and it's just not worth it. There's plenty of action out here in Bedford. We find lots of teams playing out here, and we watch them. You just drive around the county until you find a game and there you go. James used to play on a team, but he's decided he wants to work on just football and basketball, the two sports he likes better.

We actually watched a game by your school the other night—what do you think of that? I looked at the school and I got shivers, I tell you. I know some kids been trying to go to your school for years—parents can request for a black kid to go to a white school, but it has to get approved. And somehow or other, it just never gets approved. Like the paperwork didn't get turned in early enough. The next year, it'll be that the paperwork got turned in too early. The next year, it'll be that the signatures are on the wrong line. The next year, it'll be that the wrong person signed the paperwork or it got turned in to the wrong person. Mostly folks just quit trying. I've seen some families try for seven kids, and they never get one kid in that school! But they keep trying—that's how bad they want for one of their kids to go to your school. That's how much better they think your school is, compared to the black school.

And now we get to come. But I'm still shivering. Even if you are nice.

Thank you for your nice letter to my folks. You were the talk of church this week, everybody showing around their letters to parents (and Mama is pleased as punch that you called me a budding writer in your letter to her). I especially liked that you included a special note for me. Unless I'm wrong, it looks as if I'm the only one who wrote to you as Mrs. Warren commanded. That must be funny to you, as I said we all listen to her—that I'm the troublemaker—and then I'm the only one who does as told. But I think they all meant to. They just felt afraid when they put that pencil anywhere near paper. I hope you won't think poorly of my classmates. They really do try hard for a teacher.

(Thanks for the word about the one stall out of three in each bathroom set aside for the black kids— that's more than fine—we only had a one-seat outhouse for all of us to share, so this is a step up in the world for us! But maybe don't spread that around, okay?)

I had no idea it would make Mama happy to

think of me writing words down. It seems she has always taken a shine to writers! After your letter came, Mama had me help her shell peas for dinner and told me how she used to go listen to Miss Anne Spencer read some of her poetry sometimes when she had a break at her maid work with Mrs. Patsy Westover. Mama said, "You know, Miss Anne is a published poet, and she has famous men like Langston Hughes and W. E. B. DuBois at her house. You could grow up and write like her." I asked Mama to tell me more about Miss Anne Spencer and her poetry. I kept my head down, looking at those beans piling up in my bowl, the round of discarded shells growing at my feet. But Mrs. Patsy didn't like Mama going to hear Miss Anne on her breaks—not that I can see why, because it wasn't like Mama was reciting poetry when she came back—but when Mrs. Patsy doesn't like things, that means it has to stop. Mama had no more to say. She just looked at me and nodded, then said, "You could write like Miss Anne Spencer, Moon Child."

I don't know why, but poetry is one kind of writing that I'm not real interested in. . . . Poetry's like a secret that I don't understand the meaning of. But I didn't tell Mama that. I just shrugged. It seems like a good answer, to shrug, when I know I don't want to say yes to what my mama wants me to do. I gathered up my bowl of peas and slipped past the screen door into the house.

You might be thinking my mama shouldn't have to maid for a white lady when we have a farm, and I wish you were right, but our farm doesn't make enough money every year. My mama is a maid, and my granny does ironing for folks and some sewing for folks, and we all help on the farm. It works out.

James was sitting at the kitchen table, drumming his fingers on the wood. He is not a sitter, if you know what I mean—he is a mover. Not many people can be sitters when a farm has so many things need doing. One look at his face told me to keep my mouth shut, though. My brother is usually an easygoing person, but lately, he only has to hear one word to feel an anger that sets his body shaking. I went to my granny with the peas. She dumped out what I'd shelled and returned the empty bowl to me.

"That enough for supper, Granny Bits?" I asked.

"Keep shelling, Kizzy Ann," she said. "We got hungry folk to feed around here."

I must have brushed against James, because his hand shot out and knocked that bowl clear across the kitchen. Shag, always at my side, growled and moved at James. I put my hand up to keep her from trouble before I scrambled to grab that bowl. "Keep your temper," Granny Bits warned my brother. James cut his eyes at me, then mumbled a sorry my way. He doesn't usually snap at me, to be fair, Miss Anderson. Not like lots of brothers do. I suspect that thing about football has him a mite more than worried.

Yesterday I learned how you weren't the teacher at your school last year, that you're the new teacher. I heard the teacher who'd taught that grade quit because we were coming—how she wasn't about to teach no "uppity black kids." I heard a lot of teachers quit the white school and there are a lot of new young teachers there. I knew a lot of white kids had quit and were going to private schools, but I never knew that a lot of teachers had quit. Daddy is talking all the time about how Mrs. Warren had to give up her job, a job she fought to get, a job she worked so hard for, and there are teachers at your school just quitting at the drop of a hat because they won't work with a certain type of kid. I never even thought that you wouldn't want to be my teacher, Miss Anderson. I didn't see that one coming—I told you right off how much I didn't want to come and I guess I should have been thanking you for being there when I get there. Thank you, ma'am.

You asked how things are going for me, and I hate to sound like a whiner after that last paragraph, but I have to say, things are not good for me. My mother is trying too hard. She asked for some hand-me-downs for school from Mrs. Patsy. (Mrs. Patsy has a daughter a little bigger than me—maybe you know her, Laura.) Mama doesn't like to ask Mrs. Patsy for anything, but she would do whatever she has to for me.

I wish she wouldn't. Yesterday we tried on the dresses, three of them, and I'll tell you, I felt a fool.

They're frilly and satiny and my heart dropped to my knees when Mama pulled them out of the Miller & Rhoads shopping bag Mrs. Patsy had sent.

"Look, Moon Child, you are going to look like a strawberry sundae in this pink dress. And the green one will show off your lovely arms, with these cap sleeves. And oh, the white one! Like a dream." She went on and on. My mama is usually a quiet soul, so when she's prattling, you know something's wrong.

I put them on, each in turn, and they fit pretty well, with Mama only having to pin a little here and there. As I told you, we only have a small mirror, just a sliver of shine, but I didn't need to see my reflection to know how out of place I looked.

I haven't written in a while because seeing myself in those dresses (even if it was just in my mind's eye) threw me into a daze even Shag couldn't pull me out from. The dresses meant this was really going to happen. Maybe dresses aren't that much of a problem for you.

When I wore dresses to school with Mrs. Warren, I wore them because girls have to wear dresses to school and to church. Those are the rules. My granny makes most of my clothes out of leftover material she sews with, and so my dresses are just that, leftovers. I put them on of a morning and took them off as soon as I could to switch them for my work clothes. The dresses are brown or khaki or whatever material was left from what she had sitting around. They are shaped to hang down my body from the shoulders to my knees, and they cover me and that is that. I also have had other hand-me-down dresses, but never anything from someone like Laura Westover. My hand-me-downs before were just dresses from here and there — dresses from the church bazaar or yard sales, things Mama saw for sale for a nickel or something. Not like I've ever cared. I just put on whatever's there that's clean that Mama sets out. If girls could wear jeans to school, I'd wear jeans. I'm not frilly, not froufrou, not fancy. I am plain and down to business. I'm a no-bow girl, like Shag is a no-bow dog. I am not a strawberry sundae or a dream. I am just me. I am who I am. I am jeans, dirt on my hands, and my dog with me at the end of the day.

Maybe it's because of my scar. Maybe it's because I don't have a sister. Maybe it's because of how I spend my time, working with Shag on the farm. I don't feel comfortable in dresses and fancy wear and anything that's bringing attention to me. Still, I cannot make my mother's sacrifice be for nothing. After Labor Day, I will wear clothes that are not me and try as hard as I can to fit into someone else's dresses, someone else's school, and someone else's world.

I don't think this will be easy.

August 25, 1963

I hate Frank Charles Feagans. I know that's not what Jesus wants us to say, but Pastor Moore says God can read our hearts, so there's no hiding it from the Lord. Frank Charles is entirely too nosy about my dog. And his nosiness cost me a beating.

We went to Bedford City yesterday with our vegetables to sell. Saturdays are market days, and nobody can grow zucchini like Granny Bits. I helped her, just like I'm supposed to—I laid out the green and yellow gourds alternating, so the pretty colors danced together, just the way she likes. Shag lay panting in the shade under the display counter, and when Granny Bits said we could wander, I called Shag to heel and off we went.

Market is one place that is already integrated, you know. My granny has a stall right up front, where the prizewinners stay. She's won first place on those zucchini three times at the county fair, and her strawberry-rhubarb preserves win the blue ribbon year after year too. She is set up right next to the Right Reverend's wife, Mrs. Dr. Stanbridge. She is a sweet-voiced lady with the fine, downy jawline old white ladies show. Every week she hints for Granny Bits's secrets, and every week she leaves with an empty basket but a heart full of hope that she'll wheedle it out the next Saturday. Daddy says Episcopalians must be a mighty hopeful lot.

Anyhow, Mrs. Dr. Stanbridge always brings a small round bone for Shag to enjoy while we set up. Shag is used to kicks from white people, not treats, so she is wary usually, but Mrs. Dr. Stanbridge's fresh baby-powder scent is Shag's cue to peek out and ease her mouth delicately around the offered bone. Mrs. Dr. Stanbridge always exclaims about what a lady Shag is, and my dog, with her perfect manners, stands immobile while the smooth white hands glide over her coat three times.

Three is all Shag allows to folks besides family. Three trips down her fluffy fur. Then she steps back quickly and circles herself around that bone. Her crunching, her crackling, her lip-smacking enjoyment, is the background noise to our vegetable setup.

This Saturday was like any other, until that Frank Charles ran into us. I was looking over the whistles that Old Man Pickerel carves when I heard that sly Frank Charles's voice, sneaking commands to Shag.

"Come, Shag. Here, Shag. Here, girl."

Of course she ignored him.

He got a little louder. "Here, Shag."

"Stop doing that," I said. I admit, I was right snappy with my tone. I admit that. But he shouldn'a' been calling her. And then he clicked his tongue at her!

"I told you to stop that, Frank Charles Feagans."

And at that, I felt hard, tight fingers circle my upper arm. I knew enough to put my left hand up to Shag, who was already snarling. I'd been careless to speak smart to a white boy in a public place—if my dog attacked, we'd have no end of trouble.

It was Mr. Feagans, of course. He said he'd have to make me an example, and I don't think he ever took a breath, carrying on in front of everybody like I was a sneak thief when all I'd done was let his son know to stop bothering my dog. Remember how I said the ground changes when he's near me? This time those eggshells cracked under my feet.

"I'll need a switch," he said. "One of those forsythia branches," he suggested, and I knew his heart was a cold, dark thing.

Forsythia is a tricky little shrub. It looks like it'll be slight, like it won't hurt, but there is no sting like the strappy sharpness of a smartly snapped forsythia branch. After my first experience with Mrs. Warren's use of the forsythia for a switch, I gained true understanding of the wild-eyed terror of the horses who feel the whip as they pull wagons through town. And I learned a real respect for the old vet, Dr. Fleck, who abandoned a whip long ago. He refuses to coax with more than the heel of a heavy boot, a click of the tongue, and a polite request for more speed.

I forced my legs to carry me to pluck a forsythia shoot. I refused to give Mr. Feagans the satisfaction of my fear. I refused to cower.

But I cannot lie, Miss Anderson. It is a long, long walk back when you carry a switch. I dreaded what that switch would feel like, and more so, I dreaded the pleasure I knew Mr. Feagans would get from it.

I ignored the stares of the others — I've gotten pretty good at ignoring looks and the stolen glances that more polite people give me. That I can usually handle. I have to.

But I could feel anger coursing through me, Miss Anderson. Anger like James has been feeling toward that white coach. Anger like I didn't know if I could control. Anger like I shouldn't be telling you about, but somehow I can't hold away from this pencil nub.

Mr. Feagans decided it was beneath him to hold me and actually do the whipping himself. "One of your own kind should dirty their hands with your like," he said. He pointed to the crowd and singled out a huge black man, muscles coursing and rippling through his clothes. "You there, you look like the man I need."

"I'd kill the child," the man murmured. Another voice, a quiet voice, spoke up from the crowd. "I'll do your dirty work." Mr. Felix stepped forward. "I'm wiry and strong. I can hold the girl and spank her."

" 'T'isn't a spanking I want her to get, but a beating."

Mr. Felix acknowledged the task. "I can do it." He flexed his forearms, and Mr. Feagans nodded agreement. Mr. Felix grabbed me in one arm and grabbed the whip in the other. He whispered in my ear, "I'll be as quick as I can, though I can promise a little pain—it'll hurt, girlie, or he'll hurt us both worse. No way 'round it. Only way out now is through this."

He gave me one lashing for each year of age. I kept my gaze down at the dirt and pushed my hand up over and over to signal Shag to stay. She growled and snarled—she is no dumb animal, that's for sure—but she did as I signaled.

There were folks aplenty by the time he finished—black and white, old and young. Frank Charles paled out (I didn't know white folks could turn whiter, but he sure did), and I heard a few gasps from the folks gathered—gasps at Mr. Feagans's enthusiastic insistence that Mr. Felix whip harder. I also heard some nervous talk at the welts already rising on the backs of my legs, but not one being stood or spoke up.

Except Shag.

September 3, 1963

Thank you for the real journal book. Getting it today, the first day of school, with everyone getting one, is wonderful. This way I can keep writing to you, but letters would be stupid, since I will see you every day. I know I shouldn't say anything about the cost because that is bad manners, but buying one for each of us is a lot and I really thank you. And putting in our spelling words, for the spelling bees that we will have throughout the year, is a good way to do more than just our journal writing.

I've never had a journal of my own before. Even though I've learned how much my mama values my writing, she could never justify the cost of so much blank paper. Writing on the back of used paper was always good enough for my schoolwork. Because you made this a gift as well as an assignment, and one that everyone received, not a charity just for the kids like me, it sits well with my folks. I don't know how I got so lucky to have such a teacher, but I am grateful beyond my words.

I like writing things down, which I'd never done

until Mrs. Warren made me write to you. I'm not really expecting you will read all of these—everybody writing will be a lot to keep up with, but I'm still going to write like you'd read it. It helps me feel good at the end of the day. Granny Bits says this is how she feels after her prayers, but I get nervous after I pray—I do lots wrong, and what if Jesus gets tired of forgiving me?

Getting the journal was definitely the best part of the day until after school. I threw up twice on the way to school, which upset Shag no end—she kept trying to herd me to stay on the path. It's a longer walk here than to my old school, but it only took forty minutes, even with being sick.

Putting on that dress this morning was what first started me to feeling sick to my stomach. Mama picked the white one—why not start as a dream? When she smoothed that frock, her dark fingers framed against the soft white fabric, I knew it just wasn't right. I didn't belong in that dress—I didn't *want* to belong. Trying to be good to family sure can make things hard, huh?

Your building is as grand on the inside as I might have guessed. So much brick and so much beautiful carving work on a building for kids. It looks grander than my church. I'm glad we're in the first room in the hall. How would I have found us? I would wonder how you recognized me, but then, I'll bet you knew me by my scar—for once I liked it, because it was so nice to have you call my name, to hear a voice say, "Kizzy Ann," and it was like I had a friend in a strange place and I knew where to go. You have the room looking so friendly and warm and welcoming. Our names on the desks and pictures on the walls and everything. The big windows make everything sunny, which is not like our building before. Windows are expensive, I know, and the slaves couldn't do those when they built our school before. Plus, windows let the heat out. For now I like that my desk is beside the window, because I can see Shag where she waits for me sometimes out under the trees, but later I might feel pretty cold. Do you have good heat in this building? You probably do. I don't mean to start out being a complainer. I'm just nervous.

Things could have been worse, I guess. Nobody spoke to me except when you wished me a good morning. I'd expected some smart remarks, some white kids ordering me around. Of course, only four of us black kids came today, to "their" school. I heard some of the other black kids talking about how they weren't coming—even after your welcoming letters, they were afraid of what might happen. They'd heard rumors about dogs and police. They were just going to stay in their houses and see what happened.

I knew David Warren would come. He had to. His grandma is Mrs. Warren, and there is *no* way she'd allow him to stay at home.

Then the Stark twins, Ovita and Omera. They are so meek and shy that together they equal only half of a personality.

And me. None of us spoke at all. As soon as I got close enough to the building to see it, close enough to hear the chatter of students, to feel the slap of my lunch pail against my thigh, a bad taste filled my mouth and I felt my throat close tight. No words were getting past. Shoot, I was lucky air squeezed around that throat-blocking lump.

I noticed Laura Westover recognized her dress. She elbowed a blond girl beside her and whispered, then giggled. I kept my eyes lowered and my lips closed, and I was grateful that lump stopped me from saying just how mad I was.

But I was mad, Miss Anderson. I was. Even if this is an opportunity for education, like Mrs. Warren said, or a first step for our people, like Pastor Moore said, I was mad. And I don't know that I'll have that lump stopping my voice for long.

I'm not sure I want it to.

September 6, 1963

Shag was the icebreaker. After days of not being able to talk around that lump, I found it easy to open up to Shag.

She's walked me to school every day and come back for me every afternoon. But today, I guess she sensed how down I was. I've told her, of course, and I really do think she understands me, but I think she acts instinctively. Today, her instincts told her I'd need her.

She stayed.

I saw her when I peeked out the window about nine thirty. She lay at the edge of the school clearing, where the shade of the big old oak kept her cool. Her head rested on her front paws, but her eyes darted quickly. Watching for me? Watching for trouble? I can't say.

At lunch you let me go to her, and I appreciate that, Miss Anderson. You pointed her out—"Why look, Kizzy Ann, it's your friend Shag." Everybody looked. And they liked Shag, I could tell.

I joined her, there in the wind-dancing shade. The leaves rustled, the birds chirped, and Shag let her friendship and approval wash over me like a much-desired communion.

The lump in my throat melted, and I happily shared my lunch with Shag—the first bites I've been able to get down here since the first day. Her tail brushed the scattered leaves on the ground. She licked the green-bean sandwich off her muzzle and eased her right front paw onto my legs as she stretched out.

For the first time in days, maybe in weeks, I felt like I really was in the right place. My fingers settled into the soft, warm fur. And it was perfect.

Of course, life *isn't* perfect—I felt my fingers catch

in a matted area on the scruff of her neck, I pulled off two fat ticks, and I saw what looked to be dried cow dung on her back paws. But still, I had my friend and a perfect moment.

"What kind of dog is that?"

It was the first of many questions, and Laura was only the first of many students who wanted to know more about my Shag.

As fingers slid down her coat—one, two, three trips—and as I saw blue eyes and white faces look into my own, well, to be honest, Miss Anderson, I thought this might not be so bad after all.

September 9, 1963

I told my mama at dinner last night about how nice everybody was, how Shag was so wonderful, and how I should have just known she would win everybody over. I think President Kennedy should invite Shag to the White House and have her help with getting everybody to get along with everybody else. I thought things were going nice, and then, after I went out to help James with the evening milking, he told me different.

"You stupid baby. Ain't no white folks wanting to be your friend. Weren't you listening at dinner about how my JV team never gets written up in the *News and Daily Advance*? They write up every time the quarterback on the Bedford varsity team sneezes, but me and my team ain't getting anything written about us, and we're winning every damn game! We always got mentioned before. Sure, it was on the last page, but it was there." He slammed the bucket into place under Sassy, and she stomped her hoof hard. He smacked her rump and kept talking. "I'd been hoping to see some headlines with my name — *my* name. I'm the damn quarterback, after all. But since this stupid integration thing, even though my team hasn't *lost* any games, while the varsity hasn't *won* any, the paper is just not mentioning the JV team at all." He started pulling hard on Sassy's teats, and she started bawling. He turned to look at me and said, "You stupid or something?"

"But you said a lot of people, like Preacher Moore

and even the Right Reverend Stanbridge, have gone to the paper to complain."

"So what?" James said. "The editor says he prints what he wants. And he doesn't want stories about any black kids. There won't be stories about me or anybody else on the JV team, not this week or any other week. There is no JV team as far as the *News and Daily Advance* is concerned. There is *no* black football team. It is a white world." He looked at me, looked hard. "You listen to 'em tomorrow—do like I told you before, just drift on close and listen up. They won't notice you because they don't really care about you, and you'll find out what they really want. It's not being your friend, I'll bet you that, you little idiot." He tapped me on the back of my leg with his boot and pulled harder on Sassy's udder. She stomped her hooves, and Shag danced out of the way.

I listened to my brother, Miss Anderson. I looked back through my writing. My entries are filled with my fears, my doubts, my worries about how I'll be treated, how I'm different from the kids in your school. One day—one day where those kids play nice with Shag— and I had let myself believe everything is nice! I spent time thinking all kinds of thoughts about friendship surrounding us here in Bedford County and color not mattering when folks realize people are people, but then I was left wondering if James was right and I was wrong.

I got the truth today.

I eased my way near Laura and her friends, being careful not to put my interest out there for them to close the door on. I know that sometimes black folks are invisible to people like Laura Westover, and I was invisible to them today—today I was just listening. Because even though I kept telling myself good things all weekend, James's voice kept saying it wasn't right.

Dog shows. That's what they're interested in. Dog shows. Not getting to know me. Not getting to be friends.

You probably think that's bad, me listening. Granny Bits says eavesdroppers are no good, that what they're sneaking to hear will come back to bite them deep and hard. I was bothered by what they were saying, but I knew I would be even more bothered not to know.

And it wasn't right, that ideal notion of friendship and people being people.

As for Laura Westover, well, like I said, dog shows are what she and the others care about. It seems Laura's family has a prize boxer that just won second place in a dog show up in Richmond a while back. Her daddy showed him, whatever that means. I don't know much about dog shows, to tell the truth. They were talking about judging and conformation and I don't know what all. Guess I'll ask Mama to take me to Miss Anne Spencer's library soon as possible.

I feel worse than I did on the first day of school, somehow. I was nervous before. I expected white folks to make it hard. But this is worse, Miss Anderson. I made a mistake and let down my guard. I let them in, and now I feel a fool. In just a manner of days, it seems like I've gone from careful to happy to stupid, and I don't like being that. Not one bit.

I reckon it's because I'm sensitive to all of this — it seemed all special, I admit, folks liking my dog the way I like her. I got really excited. But this just hurts, Miss Anderson. And when I get hurt, I get hard. Granny Bits says it is the wrong way to get, but I can feel myself doing it all the same.

It's important to know what people who are against

you are saying. And whether you or Mrs. Warren or my parents like it or not, being at a school together doesn't change things. Those white kids aren't my friends. I know it. Folks may be pretending to offer some chances to black people, going to school together and all, but this is still a place that can see Medgar Evers shot down in his driveway like he is nothing and no one gets arrested. This is still a place where a white man can tell somebody else to switch a black girl in public and no one does a thing. You say that things are changing, Miss Anderson, but I don't see much changing at all.

September 10, 1963

That trip to town was sooner than expected. Granny Bits had some special ironing from Mrs. Dr. Stanbridge's friends in Lynchburg to deliver, and I got to pop over to the library. And I wish I could say it put my mind at ease. But, oh, I am so mad!

Miss Anne Spencer's library has a section on dogs. There are books on bulldogs, Irish setters, wheaten

terriers, German shepherds, Labrador retrievers—
you name it and there was a book on it. But not one on
border collies.

I went back to that old reliable *Encyclopedia
Britannica* and reread the little entry on border collies.
Then I went looking for Miss Anne. "You don't have
any books on border collies," I said.

She shook her head. "No."

I swallowed. I've never talked to Miss Anne much,
and, as I said before, she is a published poet. That
surely deserves respect, as most blacks aren't published, especially black women. I tried not to sound
ornery when I spoke. "You probably need to get some.
Since you don't have any. And some people might want
to read about them."

She peeked at me over her glasses. "People like
you?"

I looked her in the eye. "Yes, ma'am."

She shook her head again. "Too bad they don't
know about you in New York. Publishers in New York
decide to put out books based on what people are interested in. I suppose they don't think anyone is interested in border collies, because I can't get my hands on

one. Of course, there are a lot of books I can't get my hands on."

I didn't want to hear about what books she could or couldn't get. I just wanted to know more after what Laura had said. I guess that showed on my face, because Miss Anne gave me that look people do when they think you're getting ready to say something sassy. I swallowed up the words I'd been ready to say.

"Well," I said, "do you have anything about dog shows?"

Miss Anne took me over to the old book section, with the books nobody can check out anymore because their covers are barely hooked on or the pages are torn or whatnot. She barely touched the books as she ran her fingers over the spines, almost like a caress. She was muttering, and then her hand closed over a sage-green book and she eased it into my hands.

"This is the only copy I can get. Of course it is not new either. Be careful with it and sit right here. Don't try to put it home when you're done. Just bring it to me when you finish looking."

Librarians. I swear. They act like you can't be

trusted, like you aren't smart enough to shelve it back where it was. Like the books are more important than you. But then I thought about the way James throws a book down when he gets all frustrated with reading, and I just said, "Yes, ma'am."

I can't tell you all of it, Miss Anderson, because I was there two hours and I only skimmed all those rules. That's what it was, a rule book. From the American Kennel Club. They are *the* experts in this country, on dogs and dog shows, and everything. They have listed all the dog breeds that are recognized by them—meaning, I think, that if your dog hasn't been in America long enough or isn't good enough in some other way, you can't have your dog in a dog show. Sort of like how a dog show—the ring, they called it—isn't for just any dog.

I guess that seemed fair. I mean, the book made clear that the winning dogs, the ones picked by the judges, are examples of the breed that are closest to their own brand of perfection. And every breed has its own standards. So a soft-coated wheaten terrier must have a uniformly black nose, and it has to be large for the size of the dog. Who gets to decide "large"? That judge. So you can win in one dog show but not even get third place in another. It all depends on the judge.

To try to make things even, though, they have all these rules written down, like not having a snippy muzzle on some breeds (meaning it is pointy when it should be squared). It gets *real* particular. I don't think Old Man Hubbard's coon dog, Howler, would even be allowed *in* the ring, and he is the best tracker in three counties.

There was a lot more in there—how a dog is considered a champion if he has won fifteen points at two different major shows with two different judges, how a dog that doesn't get that champion designation is "unfinished," how a dog has to be judged while moving, not just in a stack (which is when the dog stands, posing almost), because a moving dog shows flaws that could be covered up when he's standing still. It made my head swim, I tell you.

And then I realized it didn't matter. Because the AKC doesn't recognize border collies, so Shag can't be in a dog show.

I appreciate your kind words telling me not to take things personal. But it *is* personal. When people talk together, it has to be personal, doesn't it?

"Your dog's not real." That's what that stupid Laura told me when I got to school today.

"She looks real to me," I said, reaching down to pass a cupped hand over Shag's well-shaped head. "Feels real, too."

Then she called me stupid and told me her father said a border collie was a no-account dog, not even registered with the AKC.

"I know that," I told her. "I know about the American Kennel Club. And I know that Shag could win any old dog show that lets border collies in."

"Not while she's with you, Kizzy Ann."

"You think I don't know about dog shows? For example, I happen to know that Shag is a natural at stacking."

Now, of course, you realize, Miss Anderson, that I hadn't known this for all that long, nor was I really sure that the stacking Shag did was actually correct, but sometimes the spit and vinegar just gets in me.

Granny Bits says my spit and vinegar is my curse, and she would say that what Laura told me next was my payback.

Because Laura knew what I didn't. She knew that black folks aren't allowed to participate in dog shows. That book in the library didn't say one thing about it. But Laura knew. Here's how she said it: "Read between the lines, dummy." She knew that the biggest strike against Shag isn't the fact that border collies aren't recognized by the AKC. The rule book might not say anything spelled out clear like the snippy muzzle or being registered in the United States as a breed. But it's a rule just the same, she said.

Laura Westover knew Shag's biggest problem is that she belongs to me.

I know you could tell something was wrong. And I'm sorry you were so bold as to touch my forehead to see if I was feeling poorly. I don't think you'll hear kindly about that from parents, seeing as how everybody gasped when your palm grazed my skin. I didn't mean to be pouting or anything. I just couldn't believe that my color would block my dog from opportunities. Sure, I can't go to the movies in the front door, and I can't order in a white restaurant, and I can't sit on the same school bus seat as the white kids. But I never thought my dog would be affected just because of me.

I went home and tied a bow in Shag's fur, right behind her right ear, all perky looking. I thought it would make me feel better. Shag didn't growl or show her teeth, but she let me know she didn't like it. Just like when she lets Mama bathe her in sweet-smelling shampoo sometimes, but she stands there with that hard look on her face. She lets Daddy trim her fur with shears, and she stands perfectly still, even when he doesn't do it very well. She knows, better than any of us, I guess, that she is just a farm dog. Shag doesn't care about fancy.

I slid the bow out and threw it away. Shag snugged her head under my hand, and we sat for a pretty long while. It's like she was telling me that she didn't mind about the dog show. She didn't want to stack or pose or let some judge run his hands over her fur to feel for her bones in the right places. She's a working dog who follows work commands. She's a no-bow dog. And it doesn't matter to her.

I just wish it didn't matter to me.

I don't think I'm writing in this journal anymore, Miss Anderson. No offense to you or anything. I can sit in your room, I can get to see new encyclopedias, and I can wear Laura Westover's frilly leftover dresses. But I am never going to be really equal. Not really.

October 18, 1963

Thank you, Miss Anderson, for sending my work home with David Warren, and for not saying "I told you so" about not writing in the journal anymore. Shag getting hurt just stopped everything for a while—I didn't even do my chores. (Can you believe James did them for me without a complaint? That's how serious things were.) It's been so many weeks since I could do anything but take care of her since the accident, but she is better now, and I just have to write to tell you all about it. Part of it is to get it off of my chest. Part of it is to thank you for your kindnesses. I have never asked you if you love dogs (I know you didn't have a dog, with your daddy's allergies, and your turtle, Mr. Boxster, and all, but you still could be a lover of dogs), but now I'm thinking you *must*, to understand how I could not come to school. And how I would not be able to stay away from my writing, especially after a time like I had.

It was all pretty amazing when I stop to think about it. And I'll admit to you that I was mighty scared—you see why I didn't trust myself to write until now. I sure didn't want to put my fear on the page—I thought writing it might make it more real, more likely to happen. And I could not go on without my Shag.

It was just a regular Saturday. I'd done my chores and taken Shag for a dip in the pond (I love to watch her herd those stupid geese all around the place). I was just getting started shucking corn for supper. Shag wasn't looking for trouble. She wasn't looking at all. Her eyes were closed, and tiny snores escaped her with every breath.

That ridiculous Frank Charles Feagans was waiting for Granny Bits to give him change. He comes over right often in late summer to get corn, tomatoes, and string beans. His mama just plain has a black thumb — she can't get weeds to grow, and come September, all those Feaganses are practically drooling for good vegetables. (That's what Granny Bits says. I do like fresh limas, but I pretty much only drool over fresh-churned ice cream.) Anyway, Mrs. Feagans buys from us. And even though I don't think Mr. Feagans ever asks where the vegetables come from, Frank Charles's mama sends him over to collect the vegetables only when Mr. F. is busy, just in case.

Frank Charles comes slinking across the fields. He never climbs over a fence but slides quiet like between the rails, like a sneak thief. I'd tell him no myself — I'd refuse Feagans's money — but Granny Bits says pride never put meat on the table, that money is money, and besides, none of God's children should go hungry for the harvest of the Lord.

He was inching closer to me and the pile of corn. "That dog of yours sleeps heavy," he said, pointing his head to Shag.

"She worked hard all day," I said. I was going to tell him about those geese, but I didn't get any further because as I leaned forward to pluck an ear from the pile, Shag jumped up. Mama says it was a sixth sense, but I don't know about that. All I do know is that as my hand reached into the pile of Silver Queen, Shag darted in quicker, passing my hand in a flash. I jerked back like I was on fire and screamed, "Snake!"

"Lord," Frank Charles said, backing up and stumbling. Daddy rushed from the barn, Mama from the kitchen, but they could only watch, like I did. The copperhead, its tan markings blending with the silk tassels of the corn ears, had been ready to strike. Shag took that strike for me across her right front paw. One yelp, and then she caught the snake behind its head and snapped firmly.

Shag dropped the lifeless snake, took two steps, and then dropped herself. Frank Charles amazed me. His voice didn't shake at all when he said, "Snakebite. Vet's at my farm." He ran faster than I've ever seen him move, and as I knelt beside my Shag, I saw him all but hurdle that first fence. Mama wrapped her dish towel tight around the still paw, where two sharp pricks bled brightly above Shag's nails.

Daddy pushed into the kitchen and came back with a kitchen knife. I knew he meant to use it to cut her, to let the poison drain out. I could hardly swallow around the lump in my throat.

"Hold her," he said to me, and I have never felt so strong, although Shag did not move once. Her eyes held mine, and, I guess because of her chocolate eyes, I thought of Hershey's kisses. Shag didn't allow one tear to fall, but an ocean rushed down *my* cheeks.

It seemed like just a minute and then Frank Charles was back, with Doc Fleck beside him. The old vet was huffing and puffing so hard I was afraid he'd pass out.

Shag hasn't had good experiences with white people since I've had her—she doesn't ever forget a kick—but the doctor put his hand out first and let her sniff it. I reckon she could smell all the animals he's looked after. I don't think trust has a color, but it sure *must* have a smell.

Doc Fleck looked at Daddy, still clutching the bloody knife, where he'd cut an X across those two sharp pricks. Without a pause, the doctor knelt over Shag and sucked at the poison. Then he spit and sucked again. Slowly, he eased the tourniquet towel away and massaged her, which eased the flow of blood back into her paw. Shag put her eyes on mine again, and I didn't look back at the vet to see what he was doing. Shag shuddered only once.

Mr. Feagans had come up, unnoticed until he spoke. His hands were on his hips. "I ain't paying you to tend to a darky's dog."

Silence followed his words, but I was sure I heard the cracking of eggshells.

The old white vet said nothing, just kept working on Shag. Her breathing was fast and shallow, and he slid his hands over her body. He held her as her lungs gasped air in and out, and he checked his pocket watch in time with the gasps.

"Right big copperhead," he said, looking up at Mama and me for the first time. "Good thing we're acting fast."

"Will she be all right?" I asked. And I'll tell you, Miss Anderson, my breath was coming as fast and shallow as Shag's.

He pulled a bottle of medicine out of his bag and shoved it at me. "Every day, like it says." He got to his feet and started to make his way, much more slowly, back across our land. He didn't look at Mr. Feagans, and he didn't look at Frank Charles. He only looked back at Shag, who raised her chocolate eyes to him.

"Pray," he said. "Don't forget to pray."

When I demanded she be carried to the hook rug in my room, right beside my bed, no one protested, not even Shag. She lay very still, and I stayed awake all night and listened for the little snores that proved she was still breathing.

I have given her the antivenom medicine every day. She's been very sick, I know, because she has stayed on my rug most of every day and not once has she worked the cattle.

Mrs. Warren's oldest son, Wilson, is studying to be a vet. He said lancing wasn't a good thing to do—that can lead to infection—and that, frankly, he wouldn't have wasted medicine on "such a puny dog." I figure that shows how he doesn't know beans from apple butter. My daddy says that Wilson Warren is smart and learning new things is important, so maybe lancing isn't good anymore, but Daddy will never take any of our animals to Wilson Warren no matter if he is the only vet left in Bedford County.

Doc Fleck showed up at our house three days after

he saved Shag's life. It was the only time a white man has been in my house. Daddy carried Shag down to the kitchen for the vet to examine her. Doc Fleck nodded as he felt her head and ears. He looked me up and down while he felt her stomach and listened to her heart, and then he closed his eyes. "I like a dog to have a child to love 'em and grow with. Gives 'em a job to do." He nodded at me. "Keep her busy."

He rubbed Shag's ears. She sniffed his hands and slowly, slowly licked him.

Daddy said, "We're obliged to you, Doc. Long way for the vet in Bedford."

"She wouldn't have made it," the old white man said. "Can't have a dog like this go down, not after something like what she did. Just can't have it."

My daddy swallowed. "We're obliged. Need to pay your fee."

Doc Fleck looked in my pup's eyes. "I'd not say no to a mess of that Silver Queen the girl was working on, if you've still got some that's good. The wife and I do love corn."

My father pulled his shoulders high. "I can pay money, sir."

Doc Fleck patted Shag and put his hand out to my father to shake. "Sure you can. I got money for my time out here that day, though. Don't need that right now. Could use the corn. You got some?"

The corn changed hands, and my dog and I went back upstairs.

You know, Granny Bits says that everything happens for a reason, and I guess that's so.

Anyway, I care a lot less about dog shows and Laura Westover now.

I will never shuck corn again.

I am even more confused about white people than I was before. Laura and the girls at school are mean. The vet and you are nice. Mr. Feagans is mean. Frank Charles's fast action probably saved Shag, so I guess I'd put him in the nice category even though he is annoying as all get-out. . . .

But there is one other thing I know in the category of happening for a reason for *sure*.

Shag will not sleep in the barn anymore.

Now Shag sleeps with me.

I know I've been back at school awhile since the accident. I know we've been doing spelling bees and you've
noticed I'm off my mark, losing right off the bat, and
that I haven't turned in homework, haven't written in
the journal, don't speak up in class. I'm all right, Miss
Anderson. I'm sorry I can't talk to you when you pull
me aside like you did today. I know you're kindhearted
and all, and I know there are others like you—people
like Doc Fleck—but all the signals that I'm used to in
life don't seem to help anymore. I've tried to think that
everybody is good—you be nice and the world will be
nice to you. But that just isn't the way it is, and I'm
really having a hard time figuring it all out. Who am
I supposed to believe? Who am I supposed to trust?
Shag remembers kicks and smells. She seems to
sense who she can count on by the way they *are.* And
I don't know how to talk about this to you or Mama or
anyone in person—it is all so much easier on paper.
You keep asking me to talk to you about how I feel
about the snake attack, Shag's recovery (she's fine, by
the way, honestly), about getting a group of us kids

together to talk about being here in the white school, about my scar, about how I should really think about how it all is affecting me, when all I want to do is *not* think about it. All I want to do is move on, especially from the scar, away from it and from the people who stare and make me feel like I am some sort of freak because I have a crease on my face that makes me different from them. Differences aren't welcome. Being the same is what matters. People like *same*. And I'm not the same. I'm me.

I liked it better when my life was easy. I was little, and all I had to worry about was getting dirty when I was supposed to stay clean and keeping Granny Bits happy with me. I know you worry about whether I'm bothered that the white kids aren't talking to me or welcoming me back and whether I feel okay about my scar. I didn't really expect the white kids would welcome us—this is the first year our school is integrated. I don't feel like talking to them either, to be honest. Shag's injury made me look at things different like. I think the lump in my throat, the one that kept me from saying what I felt or what I thought, is gone now, dissolved by my fear for Shag. Sometimes,

Miss Anderson, it feels like a part of me has given up on being treated equal—on seeing the world get better for me than it was for my parents or grandparents. And yet I've had glimpses, from you and from Doc Fleck, of what it *is* like to be treated equal, and I've liked it, and that is part of what makes things not easy anymore. Seeing what life *could* be like is hard. What if I'll always be coming in the back door, always be separate, always take a backseat? I don't think that will be okay with me. And I can see that it isn't going to be okay with lots of people—like James. But there are a lot of other people in the world who don't want things to change, and that will be hard for them too. I don't know what I'm supposed to do, how I'm supposed to act, when I'm supposed to speak, or when I'm supposed to be quiet—and I don't know if I even care about following the rules of the "supposed to do's." I think the world is going to be very unhappy for a while. And this is hard. Being five or something like that looks good again. But you can't go back to being five, can you?

Sometimes, when you make us work in groups—and I'm not saying which days because they all run together from when I wasn't writing to you before

Shag was hurt, and since then I've been thinking a lot about all of this and I can't make sense of it all—I've been watching how all of us treat each other. And the white kids don't really know what to do about it all either. I see them starting to be nice too sometimes. Then it's like they realize they aren't supposed to do that, like they might get in trouble at home or one of their friends might tease them or something, and they get double nasty just to make sure they don't look too nice to one of us black kids.

We start working together like regular kids, but then all of a sudden we remember, oh, yeah, they're *them*.

For instance, I worked once in a group with Frank Charles Feagans, good old David Warren, and that simpy Laura Westover. I think you had us looking up facts on ancient Egypt. Anyway, there I am, poring over the *Encyclopedia Britannica,* and Frank Charles, the little idiot, says, "Is your scar hurting today? There's a storm coming in later this evening. Sometimes people with scars can feel storms coming in their scars, and it hurts."

Great—calling more attention to my scar in front

of Laura Westover, who sat up straight and stared at my cheek in complete fascination. She, David, and Frank Charles discussed the origin of the scar for a good ten minutes while I fumed. Frank Charles was bragging— *bragging*—about his part in the whole situation.

Laura pronounced, "That is one ugly scar, Kizzy Ann, but you could cover it with makeup from the Drug Fair—they have everything. Seems to me I've seen makeup for people of your complexion there."

Frank Charles was nodding his head like his neck had a spring in it and repeating the words "There you go."

David just mumbled, "I think she's right purty like she is."

I could feel a blush spreading from the base of my neck to the roots of my hairline, and I wished so much for the ability to blend in. Curse Frank Charles Feagans and his stupid scythe.

Laura actually pushed my hair back from my face and touched my scar, saying, "If you put makeup right here," and then she gasped—she'd touched my skin. She pulled her fingers back like they'd been in an electric socket. I jerked my face back too.

All of us buried our heads in our work as if we'd done something terribly wrong.

November 2, 1963

I don't know where the money came from or whose idea it was, but a bus appeared not long ago. I use the word *appeared* on purpose because we knew nothing about it before it just . . . came. Like magic. It is slow, and it smells strongly of oil and smoke and gas, and it seems to cough and wheeze like it smokes old cigarettes, but it does save a powerful lot of steps if you are tired. I don't often ride it, to be frank. Mr. Fielder, the driver, doesn't like us black kids, that's clear—he told us the first day, "I don't care what Rosa Parks said. You're sitting at the back of the bus and that's final, got it?" We all just nodded—a ride is a ride—but sometimes I just don't want a ride that bad. Plus, there's this kid from high school, Tommy Street, who always trips every kid who walks down the aisle (don't worry, he doesn't discriminate—he does it to *every* kid, any color). I hate being tripped. Finally, if I ride the bus, I don't get to walk with Shag. The only good thing about the bus is that Mr. Fielder likes Shag. He'd apparently heard about Shag's experience with the copperhead, because the second time I got on the bus, when Shag came all the way close enough with me for him to see her, he said, "Hey, I heard about that dog, that's the one saved a girl from a snake — you that girl?"

I nodded. He stuck his bottom lip out, thinking. "Ride tomorrow, here."

The next day, when he pulled up for me, he stepped off the bus before I could get on. I backed up, as did Shag. Mr. Fielder, his suspenders drooping over his sagging tummy, knelt down in front of my dog, put his hand out for her to sniff him, and looked up at me. "Gotta let a dog smell you. They don't just trust ya automatically."

I nodded. *Got that right,* I thought. I prodded her to sniff his old white hand.

Shag looked up at me, then reluctantly sniffed the hand. Mr. Fielder turned it over slowly and opened it so she could see the good-size bone he held for her.

"Still got some meat clinging to it," he explained. "Always had me dogs, till the last few years. Miss 'em bad. Nothing like a good dog."

After I nodded to her, Shag eased the bone out of his hand and then ran off quickly. Mr. Fielder ignored my offer of a hand to help him up, held on to the side of the bus to steady himself, and got back on. I followed. "Got you one fine pup there, girl," he said.

"Yes, sir."

If I ride any other day, Mr. Fielder mutters something rude to me, but every Wednesday, we do this thing with the bone for Shag and him telling me I got me a good pup. He says exactly the same words every time. He tells me how the wife makes stew or roast every Sunday, then he launches into the good pup speech. It's gotten so Wednesday is the only day I reliably ride. I know I'll feel differently when it's really cold, but for now, I just can't do it more than Wednesday.

All I meant to do was return some library books (and I admit, I was going to see if she had some books on makeup). Miss Anne Spencer has due dates, but she'll allow you to keep books longer if you're really using them. Otherwise she considers it hoarding, which she says is a form of stealing—you're holding on to knowledge just to be holding, and that takes it away from others. Doesn't matter if no one checks that book out for ten years—if you're not using it, if you're not reading it, you are a hoarder. I didn't want to hoard.

I deposited the books at the desk. Miss Anne peered over her little reading glasses. "I expected you next Saturday," she said.

"I came today."

"But the books are not due until next Saturday," she said. "I was going to have you meet a man."

Puzzled, I looked at her. "What man?"

She pulled out a piece of paper. It was not a scrap like we have at my house, but a whole sheet of white paper (though not creamy, like what you have for letters), and she began to write.

Her script, as you would imagine, skimmed across the page. It was lovely and perfect, her *t*'s crossed and *i*'s dotted like a printing press in action. It was cursive, which I cannot read easily and certainly cannot decipher upside down. She folded the sheet and boldly penciled a name on the front: Donald McKenna.

"Take this down to the Farmers' Market. Sometimes he's there more than one Saturday a month. But I *had* told him next week."

"I don't understand," I said, taking the note from her.

"You wanted to know about your dog," she explained. "I cannot get a book for you, but I can get you a source. Fine man. He lives in your neck of the woods—near Goode. You go on, now. See that man."

I tell you, Miss Anderson, I didn't want to go see any man I didn't know. But I did have a little curiosity, I admit. And saying no to Miss Anne Spencer is like saying no to Mrs. Warren. It is just not done. So I strolled down the big hill to the market on Main Street.

There were lots of people. I didn't see a face I knew. Not that I've ever met a Mr. McKenna, but I suppose I thought I'd see someone I knew who could help me.

I was more than a little annoyed at that point. You ever pulled that hill up Polk Street? It's practically straight up, so I admit I was peeved. And then I felt a heavy hand on my shoulder. I turned and looked straight into a barrel chest and a plaid flannel shirt. I tilted my head to look up.

"You're from Mrs. Spencer," he said, and he pulled the note from my hand. I must have looked puzzled. "There are phones in the world, girl. I got a message to look for you. You're as she described. You'd not expect that a poet couldn't describe a person, now, would you?" He looked me up and down. "She says you have a dog." His blue eyes darted across the page, his head bobbing and his bright white hair going every which way. Those six words boomed out. His accent was peculiar, sort of rolling in his mouth before it burst out.

"I have a dog."

He looked at me then. Hard. His quick gaze swallowed me as I took a long look at him—his hearty head of white hair, a nose much like a beak, and white caterpillar eyebrows that wiggled back and forth over his eyes. It was clearly his turn to talk, but he wasn't saying *anything*. I waited a little longer, but the caterpillar mustache he had that matched the eyebrows didn't shift a bit. He wasn't going to talk.

I repeated, "I have a dog."

"You said that."

"She's a border collie."

"So Mrs. Spencer said."

I shut up then, Miss Anderson. I told you, I'm not walking on eggshells anymore. I didn't ask him to talk to me, so I wasn't about to scrape along trying to eke out a conversation.

We stood there then for well onto five minutes. Five minutes, Miss Anderson, is a long time to stare at a man you don't know.

He finally spoke, his loud voice filling the space around me. "Lady tells me you want to work your dog."

"I don't know what that means, 'work my dog.' She does aplenty."

He smiled at that. "Bet so. Can't stop a border collie from working."

It went on like that for quite some time, Miss Anderson, him saying three words, me adding four. Seemed to fill a long time, but all of a sudden I found I'd agreed to bring Shag to meet him one day, and I was on my way pulling that hill.

I'm wondering what I've gotten into. A white man

with a funny way of talking and a face alive with hair. Kind of feels like I'm stepping into a hole I can't see the bottom of. I'm tempted to not show up, but like I said before, I am a mite curious. And if it will help me make Shag her best, if it will help me look out for her in some way, I will go as deep as I need to go.

November 6, 1963

He has a tidy little house, I'll say that for him. At least it looks tidy from outside. Of course, I didn't go in.

Chopped wood stacked near the door, but not too close (no varmints crawling from the wood into the house). Chopping block and ax with covered blade neatly located near the stack. A shed nearby with bridles, reins, chains, and whatnot hung in an order clear to the person hanging them, every one in a particular spot. Shadows around the tools and bridles— they are hung up, or folded and hung up, the same way every time.

He sure doesn't take that much care with his hair.

He was sitting in one lone lawn chair, like he

knew I'd be coming. I deliberately hadn't said when I'd be by, had deliberately avoided a time when I thought he might be available. I wanted to miss him. I wanted him to be making repairs to an old fence or taking goods to market.

But he was there. Waiting.

Shag went to him straightaway, and that surprised me. She has never gone to anyone right away but for me. I know I sound jealous, but I'm not.

He passed his hands over her. He looked like a judge at a dog show, I thought, or at least how I imagine they look. Checking out her hip sockets, opening her mouth to inspect her teeth. "She has good conformation," I said.

His head snapped up so he looked me in the eye. "Och, girl, you one of those dog-show nuts?"

I had to admit I didn't know anything about dog shows, or at least not much.

He went back to his examination of Shag. "I don't hold with the dog-show crowd myself. It's all fine for a dog to look pretty and such, but the biggest thing is how a dog works. Dogs aren't toys. They're partners.

Don't let 'em work, you're taking the heart out of 'em. She's a good worker, I imagine." He held still then, cradling Shag's head between his beefy hands and gazing into her eyes.

"She helps me with our milk cows."

"You've not trained her, then."

I touched my leg, and Shag stood beside me again. "She helps with the cattle, I said. She comes when I want. She works."

"If you trained her, she'd do more than help. She'd think as you, knowing what needs doing by the shift of your head or the simple saying of a command." He stood up and let his hands fall to his side. "You can teach her. I will help. Every border collie ought to be trained—it makes them feel useful and satisfied."

I rubbed Shag's ear. "I don't have any money for training. Besides, she works. I'm sure she's satisfied."

He raised those woolly eyebrows. "Does she herd?"

"Oh, yes," I told him. "She herds our cows some, chickens, my family . . . sometimes she even tries to herd leaves, but they don't listen."

"Sometimes"—he kept his eyes on Shag—"dogs

like her show their frustration by working everything. She's a bright one, I can tell, and training her will help her keep her control."

"It's wrong to herd?"

"No, no. It's just that it can be a signal that they aren't getting to use all their abilities, that they're frustrated. In city dogs, they might show it with tearing up furniture, but for a country dog, it can be indiscriminate herding."

Now, I have to tell you, Miss Anderson, I just loved that new word, *indiscriminate,* but this was Shag we were talking about, so I focused back on what he was telling me. What he said made some sense, and I nodded my head. That's when I realized I'd just committed us, Shag and me, to working with this strange man. I still feel a bit nervous about it, but he did something that I believe sealed the deal. After I nodded, he whistled once, and when Shag followed, he put her in a pen with sheep and stood beside her. It wasn't like he just turned her loose — he supported her the first time she was with sheep. That felt right. It's what I would have done. So maybe this will be good after all.

I'm telling myself that, anyway.

I'm sure you've noticed how we've broken into groups to eat. Naturally, the white students eat separate from the black students, but also the boys eat separate from the girls. Even then, there are certain groups of boys who always eat together and certain girls who never eat with other girls. I'm one of the ones who moves from group to group. I don't have one particular group I belong to. To be honest, I don't really fit anywhere, but I don't *not* fit either. I'm not a loner, exactly. I can work with anybody or work alone, just depends. I sit with Shag a lot, just us, when it's still nice enough for us to eat outside. To be honest, that's my preference, but I know my mama worries if that's all I do, so I try to sit with other people, so that when I go home and she says, "Who'd you eat lunch with?" I can honestly say someone's name besides Shag's. For instance, you'll see me eat sometimes with Sarah and Mildred. They're okay, but they are pretty silly. Plus Mildred is scared stiff of Shag, even though I have told her Shag will not hurt her unless I tell Shag to or unless Mildred tries to hurt me. Mama says you can learn something from everyone in the world, but I don't know what I can learn from them. I know what I learn from eating with Omera and Ovita, the twins. They hardly say boo, except when they talk to each other in their twin language, so what I learn is Christian patience. I am exhausted after eating with them, and also more than a little annoyed. But Granny Bits says it is good for my soul to be tried by fire. Well, I am getting a good workout on my patience, that's for sure. Do you ever get lonely, eating by yourself? I'd come and eat with you, but I'm sure that would set the tongues wagging, making me look like a teacher's pet, plus you'd get in trouble eating with one of the black kids. And maybe you like to eat alone, so you can think and have a few minutes not to have to talk. Maybe I'm a trial to you. Hmm, I hadn't thought of that.

I know I've mentioned my brother to you before, but I'm getting really worried about him now. I've talked a lot about how angry James is about the football players not being treated fairly. You probably don't see a good side to James from my writing of him, I suppose. The other night I was surprised by him myself.

At dinner, I talked highly of you, how kind you've been to me, the interest you've shown in Shag. James never looked up. But after we finished the milking, we turned the cows out and walked back up the drive—all the chores done, we were in the dark and I couldn't see his face—he started talking quietly about school for him. He doesn't have just one teacher, being in high school, but it's pretty much the same, in all his classes: bad.

"Most of the teachers won't even look at us kids," he said. "They don't call our names on the roll, and you can't take tests since you didn't show up on the roll according to the way they call it. If anybody asks, they say you didn't come to class, because you didn't answer the roll. But of course, you didn't answer because they didn't call your name. I heard them talking—they call it their 'silent protest.' They say that Dr. King isn't the only one who can have a nonviolent protest. They don't give us textbooks so we can't study, and they don't call on us in class, even if we raise our hands. It's like we're invisible.

"The one time a teacher did speak to me, he said, 'Mister, they may tell me I have to let you in my room, but they can't make me teach you. So there.'"

I told James he should tell Mama and Daddy. We were almost back to the house, and I could feel Shag circling near, hear her panting as she kept close.

James snorted at my suggestion. "I thought about it, but what good would it do? You still can't make them teach us. You can't replace every teacher, Kizzy Ann. Heard about Prince Edward County? They closed all their public schools—white kids go to private schools, the ones who can afford it, and the black kids and the poor white kids get no education at all. At least here I can sit in the classroom and hear what's being taught. And there's some good teachers fighting to get the grades and rolls thing looked at—maybe these jerks can't stay in place but for so long. Just keep quiet about it and be thankful for your teacher you got."

So, thanks again, Miss Anderson. I sure do appreciate you.

November 11, 1963

Gosh, I hope you say I'm not a trial—I know you'll say you understand, even though you won't agree about the other kids. Of course you won't. You're the teacher!

I'm in *another* group with that Laura Westover. I know I'm not supposed to complain, Miss Anderson, but couldn't you keep us apart? If she tells me to get makeup to cover my scar again, I think I'll deck her! Today she had everybody in the group talking about scars. Keith showed us the back of his head.

"We were playing at College Lake, see," he said. "My brother invented this game where he throws a bottle into the lake at the same time I dive in, and I see if I can get the bottle before it sinks to the bottom. I'm a fast diver, and I can always get it before it sinks." He's so smug, I swear.

But Laura put him in his place. For once I was happy to have her around. "But not fast enough when your left-handed cousin from New York threw the bottle, right? You didn't move the right way that time, and *whack,* right across the back of your noggin!"

At least his hair covers the scar. He let us all feel it—even the black kids. It does raise up pretty nasty; his doctor wasn't near as careful as mine, but I reckon he needn't be, since he knew his hair would cover it.

Still, it's all lumpy. I thought Laura was going to lose her lunch. I was far more interested in the texture of his hair, though, to tell the truth. It's like the softest satin I've touched—reminded me of Shag's fur after her baths. I guess not all white folks have hair like it because Daisy Simmons commented on it. "Cheese and crackers, but you got nice hair, Keith," she said. "I'd give a lot to have hair like this. I wash my hair in egg whites once a week to soften mine up, but it don't feel nothin' like this. What you doin', boy?" Keith jerked his head down like it was a hot potato, and for once I wasn't the focus of the stares and the butt of the jokes. I felt a little sorry for him but was grateful all the same for someone else to be getting the attention, especially after Laura had talked about scars so much.

And the cafeteria! I didn't even realize the school had a cafeteria! The few days we haven't eaten outside, we've eaten in our room, so I just didn't know it existed. You got to eat with other teachers, so of course it was nice for you—I'm really glad. I'm sure the others liked it too—we could sit with other classes from our grade if we wanted. I sat by myself, at least until David Warren came on down and joined me, and then the Stark twins too. They asked about Shag, and it was like you knew, because you came and told us we could go check on her, and I was so worried, but of course she was fine. Still, it made me feel good to go see her then. David played fetch with her, and I didn't have the heart to tell him that's rather beneath her, but she did it anyway because she's a kind dog. And he did mean well. Of course that left me to make small talk with the Stark twins. Peesh! At least it got me out of that echoing cafeteria! It was really loud. And I missed Shag.

November 22, 1963

I cannot believe the upside-downness of the world. One day your biggest problem is whether you feel like you can work with a man whose eyebrows are alive, and the next minute your problem is that your country's president is dead. When the principal came to the door and then you told us school was closing because someone had killed the president, I thought you were just joking around. Then I could see you were crying and Mr. Glenn was crying, and I could feel a blanket of sad covering our school and our state and our nation. I hope no black man did this. I'm running home to my barn to hide, just in case.

November 25, 1963

My mama cannot stop crying. She made pancakes this morning, which she only does for funerals and birthdays. Today is nobody's birthday.

We ate our pancakes in silence, as silent as the syrup when it pours slow and smooth across the fist-size pancakes my mama stacks high. Daddy usually complains about those pancakes—he calls them two-bite pancakes—but he just swallowed one after another, barely chewing. His hand went from plate to mouth like the automatic pie machine I saw at the bus station. Pie gone, pie there, pie gone, pie there. The sad seeps over us all. It never occurred to me to walk today. I went to the bus stop automatically. When I called Shag to walk with me to the bus stop, she kept her head down the whole way. Of course I only know because I kept mine down too.

Mr. Fielder didn't say a word when he swooshed open the bus door. He usually mutters, "Watch out, darky," or something like that, but today he kept his eyes straight ahead and his mouth shut.

None of the kids moved as I walked down the aisle. Tommy Street didn't stick his foot out. Laura Westover didn't flounce her hair at me.

I eased into my usual spot right next to the big tear on the backseat and felt the silence settle around me.

You've given us extra time to write, now, as if even you can't stand to break the quiet. I can see Laura crying, but she's not sniffling out loud. And it seems the clock isn't ticking as loud as it did just Friday.

How can one man dying make the whole world hush?

November 27, 1963

After school I sat with Shag at the kitchen table. I couldn't study my spelling-bee words. I know we're supposed to keep studying on them and working for that big bee at the end of the year, but it seems pointless in light of all that is happening in the world. Shag was lying at my feet, and I was kind of tranced, smelling the hot iron from Mama in the other room and feeling weighed down by the silence. And then the quiet cracked.

James slammed into the house like a wind flying down from the Peaks of Otter — always a bad sign.

"Show of respect, my foot," he said. "They ain't canceling the varsity homecoming football game."

Mama came around the corner. She was holding a pillow cover, and her eyes were pooled up with tears. "What are you riled up about?" she said, her voice shaking as those pooled-up tears flowed over and tracked down her cheeks.

"They're canceling the JV game and the junior-varsity hop. Because of the assassination."

Mama folded the pillow cover she'd been ironing, then snapped it open and folded it again. "Sounds like a respectful thing to do, James. President Kennedy was a fine man."

Shag scrambled up and away as James clomped

over to the sink. Her toenails skittered across the wood floor, and I was reminded again of how quiet it had been. But that silence was shattered now—by Shag's toenails, by the words and footsteps, by anger and resentment leaking loud in my home.

"But they ain't canceling the varsity game, just our game. Life will go on if you're a white football player, a white cheerleader, a white high-school student. It's just if you're black that things will stop."

"Hush, James," Mama snapped, her voice soft and hard all at the same time. "You don't know who's listening—I swear even the walls have ears, this kind of thing happening and all."

My mama is flitty right now. She figures the white world was set on edge by the Medgar Evers assassination, and he was a black man—there is no telling how tender the relations between races will be now that a white man has died. No matter that he died at the hands of another white man, a Communist to boot. We had all better tread lightly, she says, and James's silence-shattering frustration is not a light tread at all.

I am afraid too, I guess. But not for the same reasons as my mama. I'm afraid mostly for my brother.

My brother is broken, Miss Anderson. He has wanted to play at the big homecoming game since forever. He stomped around in the kitchen, and then he found the noisiest piece of equipment in the barn, a tractor that just cannot find its gears, and he slammed tools around it, into it, and on top of it, all the while fuming and cussing and generally protesting the way life just will not let us get ahead.

Losing a dream is a hard and very loud business. I worry that James will never really feel better about it. I guess I hadn't realized how much Mr. McKenna and his work with Shag and me was helping me find a way to fit in to that hard world I talked about.

December 2, 1963

I've been to Mr. McKenna's again. We put Shag in the pen and stand with her. He doesn't speak, and neither do I. I like it that way, as I don't know how much I can say to him and I sure don't want to get all deep into President Kennedy or the new President Johnson or how the price of corn could affect life around here. Shag has gotten pretty good, Miss Anderson, maneuvering in and out, and I thought all was going along well.

But today was a different story. "She's been in the pen with sheep enough," he boomed when I walked Shag over to the pen where the sheep were waiting.

"What else is there to do? She already knows how to herd animals. All she needed to learn was to get used to those sheep."

"Och, girl, are you stupid, then? She's raw." He got even louder on the word *raw*. I hadn't thought he could get any louder, but *raw* erupted like a thunderclap right behind my ear.

I marched up to him, my head no higher than his chest. "She's *not* raw. She's a good dog, and she can already herd. She doesn't need you to tell her how to be a working dog."

"Prove it." This time his words were soft and slow. He narrowed his eyes, eased over to the sheep pen, and pulled the gate open. The sheep spilled out into the meadow. "Prove it," he repeated.

I stepped out, and Shag, thank goodness, stepped out with me. She started her task with no direction from me, no signal, no help. I admit, Miss Anderson, I've never had a part in Shag's work with herding. I just sit back and watch. It took her a pretty good while — about forty minutes — but she got them back into the pen and Mr. McKenna closed the gate behind them.

He was booming again as he turned to me. "Raw. She's lots of natural ability — hard to meet a border collie without it — so aye, she gets her job done. But every good dog can be better, in the hands of a good handler.

"You," he said, "you did absolutely nothing. Zero."

"I thought it was all about her and what she did."

He put his head in his hands and sighed. I've never heard a sigh that boomed, but this one did for sure. "Och, girl, perhaps you are stupid, then. She's a *dog*. You're the *master*. What she looks for is guidance so you can help her be the best she can be. Do your job and think. Lead her. Direct her. Handle her."

Shag growled, then looked to me.

I wanted to walk away. I wanted to give up. Maybe I was embarrassed or just tired — I don't know. I wanted to just plain leave it all behind me.

But I thought of Laura Westover dismissing Shag

and me. I thought of Mrs. Warren knowing I stand up for things I need to. I thought of Shag, looking up at me, counting on me to help her be her best. And I thought of James, and all the bad that comes when you don't have enough to believe in to make you care.

"Teach me," I said. And I'm hoping he will.

December 10, 1963

It isn't easy, Miss Anderson. First, Mr. McKenna had me learning the history of border collies. I won't bore you—you would be bored, Miss Anderson—but I'll tell you that border collies are among the smartest of dogs, and they have helped people with herding for a long, long time. Just like people, there are some who stand out, and one of the most famous is Shep. He was a border collie who amazed Scotland with his talent combined with a demeanor that allowed him to work easily for his master.

Shag also has a good attitude, at least for working with me. She doesn't, however, take to just everybody, so that could work against her in a trial, which is what the border-collie world has. Yes, it turns out that something like dog shows exists here too. You can win the big prize or the second place and so forth, but it's not about how your dog *looks*. It's about how your dog *works*. This seems the better place for Shag and me. Still, I think the dog may need to take commands from a judge, and Shag is none too happy about taking commands from anyone but Mr. McKenna or me.

"I've written a list of commands for you," he announced one day. He held a walking stick, and he had a pink tinge to his face as he shoved the paper into my hands. "It's written in the language of sheepdogs and shepherds. You'll need to be learning that. Learn it by heart—once you and Shag know them together, you'll truly be a pair." He said this as he marched toward the distant meadow, filled with his white woolly sheep.

I looked the list over, and, Miss Anderson, I have to tell you my eyeballs clear jumped. "This is a bunch of nonsense. What does 'go by' mean? And 'outrun'?"

Mr. McKenna gripped his walking stick so tight

his knuckles turned white as his hair. "The language of dogs. The language of Scotland. And I'll appreciate you saying nothing negative regarding it." He stared straight ahead, his gait eating up the ground to the meadow.

I was trotting to keep up. I'll have to admit that it is hard for me to apologize. But apologize I did. "I'm sorry. It's just I don't understand."

He smiled at me, a crack in his demeanor for one split second. "We all have things to learn, girlie. You're not alone in that."

He cleared his throat and explained as we neared the gate to the meadow. "'Go by' means you want your dog to circle to the left of the herd and drive them to the right a bit. We need you and Shag to work almost instinctively, but I do say *almost*, Kizzy Ann. Because the border collie has instincts closely tied to the wolf's, and sheep killing is an instinct we never want a border collie to experience. It is hard to bring them back once they've been to the edge. A dog like that has no place then on a farm, and without good work, your dog is lost."

I looked at Shag, her easy glide beside him, her ears perked, alert to the sheep, and her fur almost standing on end, so ready was she to get to work.

We spent hours, then, Miss Anderson, hours having me recite a command and Mr. McKenna leading Shag through the action that corresponded.

Now Shag and I are figuring out the basic commands. I know how to send her left, right, and one of the possible ways to get her to bring in the sheep. It's called an outrun, going in either direction out and around the sheep, to get behind the flock. The trick is for Shag not to go straight at them, but to move in an arc so she ends up behind the sheep. At this point in my learning, I need to try to work with Shag so the flock stays between the handler and the dog. Mr. McKenna says that doesn't always happen, and he also says the shape of the outrun is one of the things judges look at in a trial, but Shag and I aren't ready to worry about any of that yet.

Anyway, she gets back there, and at a certain distance she uses what Mr. McKenna calls her eye stalk to get the sheep moving toward the pen. It's kind of hard to explain, but she has to stare them into moving.

She controls them with no movement. An eye stalk is really important, and the sheep's response determines if the dog has a strong or weak eye. Nothing I do matters here. You won't be surprised, I'm sure, to know that Shag has a strong eye.

"Your dog is saving you, girl," he said today after Shag got the sheep into the pen. "You've learned up to a point, I'll give you that, but then you break down and she has to revert to instincts alone. Not fair to the wee dog, treating her like that."

"I'm trying."

He looked at me, up and down, and I was amazed to see his gaze soften. "Och, I know, girl. But you must do better. Think like a dog, or pretend the sheep are yours, or do whatever it takes, but you've got to start improving, or your dog will give up on you and all is lost."

I know that could never happen, Miss Anderson, never. Shag would never give up on me. Still, I'll have to work harder. I can't let Shag down.

I'm talking about how I'm not giving up and won't let Shag give up, but I think James has. The air is gone out of James. Oh, he's still breathing and all. He goes through his day, he does his chores, but it's, I don't know, it's like there's no life in him. He doesn't tease me, he doesn't get mad when Mama makes him get up for early milking, and heck, he doesn't get mad about *anything* anymore. The JV team finished up their season (finished first in the state), and he just sort of wilted. I'm living with the ghost of my brother. I never thought I'd want a good punch from him, but I'd take that James any day over the James who is sliding through life.

December 13, 1963

I went to Mr. McKenna's today. We worked on my understanding of Shag's balance point. It's a *very* precise thing, and it will make or break us. It is how well she can read the sheep and understand which direction they'll move in. The balance point varies dog to dog. Mostly it's genetic, but I have to be aware and keep Shag controlled, commanding her to slow down or get down, or whatever it takes to stop her from shifting too early to her next balance point. I have to teach her a nice pace so things don't turn into a chase, and I might have to get her to lie down quickly to keep distance between her and the flock. It all comes down to how well the handler knows her dog's behavior and controls it.

That really was fascinating—but here's the part I want to tell you. When we took a break, Shag went to the shade. Mr. McKenna penned the sheep where Shag and I had put them, and then he said, "You could invite your friend to join us, you know."

I stared at him. "Friend?"

He pointed toward the west woods. "Him."

I looked, just in time to see a blur of movement. "I don't know who that is," I said.

Mr. McKenna's eyes got big. "He's there most every day. Figured he was with you. He watches, applauds sometimes."

Suddenly, I knew who it was. That darn Frank Charles Feagans.

I could see him, then, crouched behind a bush. I swear, his scruffy red Keds were like a red flag waving. I stomped over, Shag skittering beside me.

"Come out."

He didn't move.

"For Pete's sake, come out, Frank Charles."

"You can't see me."

I leaned over the bush and stared at his head. "Yes, actually, I can. Your cowlick is pointing toward the schoolhouse, and you are as easy to see as I am."

He stood up and stepped out, crackling dead leaves under his sneakers.

"You're following me," I said.

"Am not."

I sighed. Honestly, it was like talking to a two-year-old. "Yes, you are. I'm here. You're here."

"Following Shag. Not you."

Following Shag! What? This wasn't annoying anymore. My dog, *my* dog, the one thing that matters most to me, the one being who *is* my world. How dare this moron come near her? This felt threatening. His father beat me . . . now what would he do to my dog? I grabbed Frank Charles's coat collar and jerked him close. "You will *not* hurt my dog."

His eyes widened, and he shook all over. "I'd never hurt her. *Never.*" His voice shook with the sureness of his word. "I just, well, I mean, I . . . I can't stop looking at her. She's so, well, clever and quick." He stumbled out of my grasp. "Pa won't let me have a dog. Says they'll spook the cows, you know."

I dropped my hands and touched Shag's nose. She was right there beside me, like always. But she wasn't growling at him. I decided to stop growling too.

"She is pretty amazing," I admitted.

"I been watching you," he said. "Not you, I mean, her. She's getting really good at making the sheep go where you want, it looks like."

I hadn't heard Mr. McKenna approach, but I knew he was behind me when his shadow fell across us. "You'd see more if you come on closer. Might as well. You're here anyways."

And just like that, Frank Charles Feagans was a part of my training of Shag.

December 19, 1963

I've never made a gift for Christmas at school before. There just never was any money for Mrs. Warren to buy materials for that. I always make gifts—that part isn't new—but not at school. I don't rightly know if that pot holder will be of much use to Mama (mine turned out right sad compared to Laura Westover's), but the colors are bright and she does love colors.

And getting a present from you. . . . Gosh. Sometimes Mrs. Warren gave us a peppermint, and I heard about a year when she got all her seniors a book apiece, but that never happened when I was in school, so this is really exciting. They were all wrapped so pretty too. We wrap with old grocery sacks that we decorate usually—this store-bought paper is especially fine. I know some of the others weren't excited. I guess you heard Laura Westover say, "Oh, another book." But I'm really grateful. We only have the Good Book at our house, so it will be nice to have another, whatever it is. And I'm not going to unwrap it until Christmas morning, even if I do know it's a book.

We used to have a party at school, but I knew the white folks weren't going to let that happen. My mother makes most of the meals that are served to Laura and her family, but if I brought something made *at* my house, none of the white kids would eat it. They trade lunches all the time, but never with us. Sure, I understand that cold potato cakes and a hard-boiled egg doesn't appeal to everybody, but who could turn down my mama's oatmeal cookies?

Anyway, I'm glad to have some days to work on finishing my gift for Shag. It's a braided collar, and the plaiting takes me forever and a day! It was hard, screwing up my courage to ask Granny Bits to help. I've often pooh-poohed her handwork, so admitting that I needed her help to make gifts was tough. It took me three days to work up the nerve. I went to her after she'd finished her morning prayers—she's often her most approachable then, when she's thinking about the blessings the Lord has given her. Can't wait too long or she's on to thinking about how James and I annoy the heck out of her. I eased up next to her, put my hand on her arm, and asked, "Granny Bits, I believe you know just what I need to learn to make Christmas gifts." She was not taken in by the buttering up, but she liked it.

"Knew you'd need me sooner or later," she said. Now, I suppose you might think that's pretty gruff of her, but really, for her that's mild. She even talked to me about what exactly I'd like to make. I didn't have any ideas for you, being as you're a white lady and all, but Granny said, "She's same as other ladies, liking fine things for her house." So we tatted the armchair cover you got. I hope you like it—those cow hitch knots aren't easy, and Granny Bits didn't let me get by with any that were less than fine. "She's an educated lady—teachers deserve your full respect and your best efforts." That's what she said every time I tried to convince us both that you'd be happy with my effort, even if it didn't look perfect. "Good effort doesn't dress up a chair." You'd think the president was coming to see you, the fineness she felt your chairs had to have. But I needed her to get me started. She may fight the arthritis, but she sure knows what hands should do to create.

I thought she'd fuss about the collar for a dog, but she just nodded. That plaiting was a bit easier than the tatting, maybe because Granny Bits didn't worry too much about a few little mistakes. Still, it took five days' finger work, even if it isn't the prettiest thing you ever saw. I figure Shag will appreciate the effort. Part of me worries that she won't like it at all—after all, she is a no-bow dog. But all the pictures Mr. McKenna showed me of border-collie champions showed dogs with collars.

I was going to put a gold tag with Shag's name engraved on there when I finished making it. But I've decided to use the little bit of money I have to get something for James. I know before he was very mad and very loud and I was worried he'd do something crazy like yelling at that white coach, but now you know how awfully quiet he's been, like a shadow. Now I'm kind of scared the crazy thing he might do won't be against someone else but against himself. He's still so different—sometimes he's talking and a part of us, and other times it's like noon for shadows . . . you know he's there but you can't really see him. He just moves through chores, sits through classes. His body *is*, but the real him is gone. It's like he is so sad he can't find happy.

Maybe a present won't help; I can't buy a different world. But it's all I can do. And I *have* to do something.

Well, it wasn't our finest Christmas, but it's done. James smiled some and seemed to like the new work gloves I gave him. He even said thank you, which was two of the five words he uttered all day.

Everyone loved the gifts I made at school—Granny Bits just raved. You'd think she'd never seen pot holders and dream catchers made out of yarn and Popsicle sticks. It was nice, though, to see my family happy and to know I helped make that feeling.

Shag and I went outdoors after church ended. Does your church have a special service on Christmas Day? Ours is quite long but not boring like church sometimes can be. We have lots of singing and then our pageant with the little kids pretending to be shepherds, angels, and baby Jesus. We finish with a rousing rendition of "Hark the Herald," which is my most favorite Christmas song ever.

Shag and I walked sort of haphazardly, our legs for once not gobbling up the miles. Even though the Christmas service is a nice one, sometimes being cooped up in our house and then church is just overwhelming to me. I feel my muscles scream to stretch and my lungs ache to open on air that isn't trapped and stagnant, overflowing with the rich aromas of corn bread, country ham, and corn pudding and the pungent odors of Pastor Moore's talcum powder that he slathers over himself and Old Lady Drinkard's stale and slightly mummified "scent of gardenia" perfume mixed with the runny eggs she spills on herself every church day. I always need to get out and be alone on Christmas for some time on my own with Shag, and we take our time, meandering around until I can look back into the family faces. I know this seems a strange way to feel about a holiday, but Christmas sometimes settles in my chest until it feels like I will pop.

My walk took us out a couple of miles, and on our way back, we came near Frank Charles's land. I wasn't looking for trouble, and I sure wasn't looking for Frank Charles. I just wanted a walk and some space of my own, and the creek I followed happened to close in near the Feaganses' meadow.

Then something caught my eye, a sliver of shadow, I suppose, and I instinctively called Shag to me. I ran toward the shadow with the lightest tread I could manage. As I closed on the spot, I heard voices, angry and shouting. I don't know why, Miss Anderson, but I started this strange shaking inside, like my whole being was afraid or chilled to the bone. I got myself to a grove of mossy-footed oaks and huddled there, waiting for the shaking to stop. Shag crouched beside me, and I realized why I was shaking. It was James's voice I heard.

He was shouting at some of the Feaganses' cows—three scraggly cattle that now found their way blocked by James, Cabbie Simpson, and Montgomery Watkins. The boys were waving knives, yelling at the cows, and herding them toward the small smoking shed where the Feaganses keep their curing meat. Those cows were looking all spooky, the whites of their eyes showing like the petticoat that always pokes out of Granny Bits's dress. They could take out that shed in a heartbeat—no lie, Miss Anderson—and there'd be hell to pay then, sure enough. The beating I took at the order of Mr. Feagans was nothing to what he and the law would do to three black boys causing trouble.

I was still shaking like when I had that scythe fever, but I felt like I had to stop things. I gave Shag a command to come by, and together we moved out of the stand of trees. I took to one side of the cows and sent Shag to the other, but I can't tell you what exactly happened after that. I gave commands and I saw Shag follow, but I heard shouting and calling in my ears, muffled—things all blocked up in my head, like when I had the cold settle there last winter. My hearing wasn't the only thing blocked. I moved, but it was like I was walking though molasses and I knew I wouldn't be able to stop those cows from hitting the shed. I don't know if it was that I wasn't sure of what I was doing; I don't know if it was the boys getting between Shag and the cows. I simply don't know what went wrong.

At the last minute, I had the presence of mind to call Shag out of the way, and she pulled out right before the shed would have collapsed on her. The cows just hit the shed and sheered off as the shelter collapsed. Their bawling cries filled the air, so loud, shaking the sky, and it seemed like people should have been able to hear all the way into Bedford City and downtown Lynchburg. I looked back and thought I could see between the slats of the shed as it fell, see the meat falling into the pit where the fire is kept stoked, see a winter's worth of food lost. I heard shouts and cries from far and near, and I rushed to the safety of the trees with Shag called to my side. I know I must have imagined this seeing— I couldn't really have seen between the slats—but I would have sworn on a month of Sundays that I'd seen it. It is that vivid in my mind: hams hanging, falling down, down into a pit, while screaming cows slam into falling boards as they hit the ground.

The cattle continued to mill about, stomp the ground, and moo loudly, but the act of knocking the structure down seemed to have taken most of the scare out of them. Suddenly I saw Frank Charles in the middle of the cows. Where had he come from? He was calming them, easing them, and then he looked me straight in the eye. I wish I could make this a clear scene for you, but I lived it and I cannot make it clear for *me*, so I don't see how I can make it clear for you— it is a jumble of moments, a mass of minutes that happen like blinks of an eye, one and then another and then another. I don't know what happened to James, or his friend Cabbie or that Montgomery Watkins, but after I heard their shouts and saw them start the cows toward the building, I didn't think of them again, so sure was I that Shag and I could stop things.

But we didn't. I didn't do anything but risk Shag at that building collapse. I think I might have made things worse.

Mr. Feagans rushed up, and I pulled my head back into the bushes and gave Shag a signal to be still. My heart felt like it was pounding through my chest, and my mouth went dry like after I've run my hardest.

"Gol darn, boy, who's messing with my cows?" Mr. Feagans yelled, pushing a hand through his hair.

Frank Charles eased his fingers onto Bessie and put his back square between me and his pa. "I, uh, I spooked 'em. Didn't mean to, Pa. I just cracked a stick and it sent them into some sort of nervous spell. I didn't mean to, really."

Mr. Feagans lashed out and smacked Frank Charles full on the mouth. Shag started to rise, but I stopped her. There was no sound at all. Frank Charles put his hand to his cheek and mumbled "Sorry" over and over.

The cows followed Mr. Feagans's sharp command,

and he started behind them. "Come on, boy. Got to get some bags, try and save some of that meat. God a'mighty, but you're one sorry excuse of a son."

Frank Charles took one deep breath but didn't look back. I know he saw me. I know he saw James. And now I've told you.

What will happen to us, Miss Anderson? What will happen to us now?

January 3, 1964

Frank Charles is a surprise.

I had to snatch a minute with him on the way home—no easy feat with that nosy Laura Westover. Of course, she thinks Frank Charles is pretty low on the list of important people, so she doesn't do much with him for the most part. I cornered him where he cuts off the path to head home.

"What are you going to do?"

He turned to me with a blank look on his face.

"Do?"

"I know you saw me. What are you going to do?"

He shrugged. "Nothing."

I can't stand worrying about stuff like that, waiting to see. I pushed it. "I know you're going to tell. Let's just get it over with."

"I'm not doing anything about anything," he said. "We got most of the meat."

"And the building?" Shag was circling us and watching closely.

He shrugged again.

"Why are you taking the blame for me?"

He shook his head. "Wasn't you. I saw your brother and those boys."

I wanted to lie, Miss Anderson, but you know I'm pretty bad at that. I kept looking at him.

He shrugged *again*. But then he continued talking. "I don't really know. Seems like things just got out of hand. I'd gone up there hoping to run into Shag, and I heard your brother talking. At first he sounded—I don't know—sad or something. And then he started sounding mad, and then things got all mixed up. I get mixed up sometimes.

"But my pa wouldn't understand that, about James. Or me, really. He doesn't seem to ever get mixed up. He always knows what he thinks." Frank Charles wouldn't look me in the eye, but he stared at Shag. His hands were going in and out of his pockets. "He tells me what I should think, what's right and wrong. And he's my daddy, you know. But sometimes, I just don't know what's right. He'll do something and it feels, um, ugly or mean or something. I get mixed up then. I just don't always know what's right. You know what I mean?"

I knelt and slid my hand down Shag's warm, soft back. "I know."

He sat down in the dirt and put his hand toward Shag. He paused and looked at me, his eyes questioning and hopeful. I gave a little nod, and Shag shuddered just a little as Frank Charles Feagans, the boy who made me Moon Child, the boy who's protecting my brother, the boy who surprised me more than I can say, passed his hand one, two, three times down the length of Shag's body, drawing comfort from the dog he admires almost as much as I do.

I didn't say thank you but I should—I suppose you aren't going to tell on James or me. Your little note in my journal, about all being well, makes me believe you kind of think like Frank Charles. Thank you. How many times will I end up saying thank you to you in this one little journal? And when you thanked me, I guessed you figured that I'm Frank Charles's friend now and well . . . I guess I am.

James stopped me when Shag and I came back from Mr. McKenna's. "Went over and helped Mr. Feagans fix the shed today." He kept stacking wood, but he looked me in the eye.

"I'm glad."

"Thought a lot, after you jumped in, trying to help. And you didn't tell. I'm not sure why you'd do that for me."

I nodded. "Seemed the right thing to do."

"Sometimes I don't know if I understand you," he said, pulling another log out of the chopped pile and onto the stacked one. "Oh, I . . . I didn't tell him it was me what did the damage."

"Probably the smart thing," I said. "Frank Charles took the blame."

"Frank Charles? That little kid who comes over for vegetables sometimes? Why would he take the blame?"

What could I say to explain, Miss Anderson? I thought for a minute, but all I could come up with was "I think he just felt it was the right thing to do."

"Sometimes I don't reckon I understand white people, Kizzy Ann."

"I think it's just understanding people, James."

January 15, 1964

I tried to get Frank Charles to hire me. I had to be out of my mind, when I think of it. His family doesn't have any extra money, so why in the world did I think he would have anything to spare? I've been studying on it quite a bit, looking through your *Encyclopedia*

Britannica and the use of makeup in ancient Egypt, and I thought if I could just get some money, I might be able to go to Drug Fair and try a few things to cover my scar. I don't know what I could do for Frank Charles's family, but who else could I work for? Anyway, I guess he figured things out, or I don't know, but what amazing friends I have . . . because Frank Charles told Mr. McKenna, who went to Drug Fair, and he bought makeup for a black woman! I sure would have liked to have been in the store when that happened—this very white-haired, pale-skinned Scotsman going into the Drug Fair in Madison Heights and discussing which makeup products to buy for "women of dark complexions." HA! I don't know how he did it! Or maybe he didn't discuss anything with anybody, because he basically had everything under the sun in that Drug Fair bag. I guess he just bought everything they had in the store and asked no questions at all. Frank Charles brought me the bag. He caught me by the stream and said, "Here you go. Mr. McKenna says you look fine, but if this'll make you feel better, then take it," and he shoved the bag at me. He was red in the face, and he ran off faster than I've ever seen him run.

I feel a fool, Miss Anderson, but I'm also excited. Maybe this will be the answer. I know I haven't said much about it in here. In fact, I've deliberately *not* said much about it in here. I spend nights looking at the moon and trying to figure out how I feel about my face, about my name, Moon Child, about my scar. Knowing my face will never look as it did before, I finger my raised skin. How is it when you know you will never be the person you were before? Does Keith dive into College Lake with the same abandon now that a bottle sliced into the back of his head? When Shag saved my life, I was not the same Kizzy Ann I was the day before. When my brother got into trouble in the woods, I was not the same as the day after, nor was he. When Caroline Kennedy woke up on November 23, she was not the same girl she was the day before, even if her face was as pretty as the day before — her life is a lot better than mine in a lot of ways, but it is also a lot worse.

I know people look hard at me. I'm not stupid. Pretty girls get things that ugly girls don't. But smart girls get things too. And I am smart. Anyway, I pulled out the makeup to look at it, but I realized that I don't know what to do with it—and I am smart enough to know that if you just put makeup on without knowing about it, you don't end up looking good. You end up looking worse. This is not something I can ask my mama or my granny about. I plan to go to the library as soon as I can. Let's hope Miss Anne Spencer has more books on makeup than she has on border collies.

January 30, 1964

I went to the library—not today, but I'm just getting to write today. There is a lot more to a poet than you think! Miss Anne Spencer had books on makeup, and she let me look at them, but then she invited me to her study for tea. I didn't want to go, but how do you say no to a force like Miss Anne Spencer? You don't. I pored over the books on makeup. I have to admit they were overwhelming. Lots of diagrams that looked like you need a degree in engineering to understand, at least it seemed to me. Who would think putting on makeup would be so danged hard? But the books she pulled for me were about masking scars, not just your basic makeup, and I started getting nervous. They were for people with severe scars. Like me. It seemed so complicated. I put the books on makeup back on the shelves and went to her study. She had tea things ready for us. She sipped her tea and then she "cut to the chase." That's exactly the way she said it.

"Let's cut to the chase, Kizzy Ann. You're looking at these books on makeup because you want to cover yourself up, am I right?" She took a delicate sip of her tea.

I nibbled a scone. At least I think it was a scone. I don't really know. I'm not too knowledgeable about tea etiquette, as you might expect, Miss Anderson. "Yes, ma'am," I said.

She tilted her head to the side and looked me over. "I don't know if your scar will fade, but it doesn't seem to dominate your countenance."

Another new word. *Countenance*. Read it in the Bible before, but never heard it in everyday talk. I wrote that one down as soon as I got out of there, even if I had to put it on the palm of my hand, as I had no paper. I said, "Well, to look at the reactions of the people around Lynchburg, you'd think it dominated my countenance. If by that you mean it is the main thing they see when they look at me."

She smiled. She has a real pretty smile. I don't see it often, as I rarely make her smile. I am often a nuisance to her. She set her teacup down. "Kizzy Ann, I'm not in your situation: I have no scar. But I know two people who were scarred by life in . . . not dissimilar ways. Let me tell you about them."

Hmm. My first thought was *Can she really know two people who had severe scars? That's pretty many. But then I guess a librarian knows a lot of people.* My next thought was *I've probably missed some of what she is saying and that is rude, and Granny Bits would skin me alive if she could read my mind, so I'd better stop thinking and start listening.* Miss Anne must have known I wasn't paying close attention, because she put a hand on my hand and looked into my eyes. Her voice was soft.

"My cousin was beautiful like the flowers in my garden, Kizzy Ann. When she was nineteen, she was trapped by a fire in her bedroom and though she escaped through the window, her neck and the right side of her face were damaged. Laura couldn't recover from the sad fact that when she looked in the mirror, she no longer saw her own face but the face of a stranger. She retreated from people and wouldn't be seen. She wrapped herself in scarves, even though her skin hurt to be touched by any fabric. Sometimes I think I revel in my flowers to be close to the beauty that was a part of her.

"I knew another touched by tragedy, but rather than letting it shape her life with sadness, she made her own way. She was burned differently. More of her body was involved, and so there was *more* scarring, but it was less severe. Still, when you looked at her, you knew she'd been in a fire. You knew she'd had . . . damage."

"People stared."

Miss Anne Spencer swallowed, then nodded slowly. "Yes, Kizzy Ann. People stared. A lot. But my friend just didn't care. No, that probably isn't right. I suppose she did care, although she never said. She just went ahead with her life. She didn't wear lots of makeup. She didn't stop doing what she wanted to do. She went ahead and lived her life. Because she had things she wanted to do. And she did them."

Miss Anne picked up her teacup then and took a sip.

"I think you, Kizzy Ann, have a choice to make with your life. Do you want to be like my cousin, do you want to be like my friend, or do you want to fall somewhere in between? It seems to me you are a young lady with a whole lot of life to live and much to offer the world, but then I'm not the one living your life."

I sat there a few more minutes, holding my tea. Then I put it down and stood. I didn't know what to say, but then I thought of something.

"Miss Anne?"

"Yes, Kizzy Ann?"

"When you're reading your poems . . ."

"Yes?"

"People stare, don't they?"

"Why, yes, child, yes, they do."

I don't agree with Miss Anne Spencer that her cousin and her friend had scars from similar circumstances to mine. In my opinion, a fire is nothing like a scythe that slices through flesh. Maybe a fire that is set on purpose, but what she described was accidental fire, the kind of flame that rises out of dying embers left smoldering in the fireplace kicked up by a sudden gust down the flue, embers that dance and catch a curtain and climb quick and wild. That kind of fire you can feel sorrow for, you can feel sadness seeping into your bones, but I don't think you would feel the raw anger I felt toward Frank Charles Feagans.

I know you're surprised to read that. I'm surprised to write that. I've never even told myself that, so how could you know? I've been friendly to him—I've shared my dog with him, for Pete's sake—but I was so mad at him . . . well, angry, which I think of as a much *bigger* emotion than mad. But Granny Bits says anger is wrong, especially when things are accidental.

And it *was* an accident. Frank Charles had no intent in his swing. His movement was distracted by the agility of my dog, my amazing, incredible Shag. And I can admit to you, here in my journal, I feel such guilt still feeling my raw anger toward him—and I do still feel some tiny bit of anger toward him, Miss Anderson— even though I think of him now as my friend. I am amazed to think he is a friend to me. I suppose I haven't truly forgiven Frank Charles. I don't honestly know how people forgive and forget, as we are told to. I *say* I do—Granny Bits insists on it—but I seem to hold on to my grudges and remember who said hurtful things. In fact, I can quote them back, almost verbatim, sometimes months after they happened. And that's just little piddly conversations . . . so how in the world will I ever shed this ugly thing filling my heart?

February 4, 1964

Today I ate with Omera and Ovita Stark. They have started to talk a little to me, if no one else is around. Shag ate over by my side, since Ovita in particular is a little scared of her. They sounded like chickens, clucking on softly to each other about this and that, about nothing really. But then they started talking about clothes. You know I don't care a fig about clothes, Miss Anderson. But Ovita said, "I hate going to try on clothes."

I admit I hadn't really been listening for a few minutes. I'd been feeding sandwich scraps to Shag and just half listening to the sound of their conversation. But it was clear they were waiting for me to say something, so I said, "Yeah, when Mama pulls one dress off and I'm standing there by my bed with chill bumps on my arms, hoping James doesn't get the bright idea to walk in on us, I just want her to hurry up and get that next dress on! Good thing my granny can't make but two at a time!" I laughed, nervous like, because they were staring at me like I was talking about weird things.

"Oh, that's right," Ovita said. "You don't get your clothes at the store. You don't know what it's like."

I just looked at them.

They looked at each other. Omera took a deep breath, looked at Shag (I don't know why), and then said in a whisper, "It's humiliating, Kizzy Ann. Folks like us aren't allowed to try on clothes in a dressing room. The owner of the store doesn't want the clothes to actually touch our skin. He says . . . he says he can't sell the clothes we don't buy if they've touched our skin. So, we either have to just pick some-thing off the rack and buy it or we put it on over our own clothes, right there in the middle of the store, and you have to wear long sleeves and gloves to try things on, so your skin and 'body oils' don't 'soil' the clothes."

Ovita made a face. "Like our blackness will rub off on the clothes. Like we're dirty."

I have never been so glad that my granny makes my clothes. I have never been so glad that my mama accepts hand-me-downs.

February 11, 1964

Okay, you have to promise not to tell anybody anything about this, Miss Anderson. I shouldn't tell you, I don't guess, but this journal has sort of become where I put down everything I think, everything I work through in my head and my heart. Today I was working Shag and practicing commands like always, and I heard this voice, little at first and then desperate, calling for help. And I knew, not at first, but then I knew, that it was Frank Charles. Shag had already started running toward the voice, but then I kicked up and ran too. We'd been over toward that edge of the property, the Feaganses' side—we are neighbors, after all. I guess they were collecting kindling or something. I think I noticed some firewood, but really, all I remember seeing was Frank Charles kneeling next to his mother, who was lying on the ground and shaking like Sassy, our cow. Remember how I told you she'd started having seizures—epilepsy, you know? Well, there Mrs. Feagans was, shaking, and Frank Charles was screaming at her, and he took her shoulders and I guess he was going to pull her to sit up.

I don't know why, Miss Anderson, but I sort of took charge. I put my hand on him and just told him no in a calm voice. I told him to leave her be, and I turned her on her side and talked to her in a low voice, like I do with Sassy. I think I might have seen this at my church once, when I was little, now that I think on it—a girl in my Sunday school class who stopped coming when her seizures got so bad, but before she stopped coming, the teachers just made us all sit quiet and treated it all very matter-of-fact and rubbed her forehead and talked her through her spell. I remember they told us that people in a seizure often spit up or wet themselves and they might need to sleep afterward and might not remember things for a while.

So I guess I just remembered all of that in a way, and did that with Mrs. Feagans. I tried to keep things calm for her and Frank Charles. Shag stretched out right next to Mrs. Feagans, up against her back, and we just sort of stayed with them for a while and made it a time of peace as much as we could. When she came to, I was holding her hand and stroking her hair, and we talked. I'd sent Frank Charles for a blanket—it was February, after all, and we didn't want her to get chilled badly. Of course, I ask you to keep this quiet because epilepsy is one thing for a cow and quite another for a family—I didn't ask if this has ever happened before with Mrs. Feagans. It is none of my business, and I know Frank Charles wouldn't want me to be sharing it around with everybody. He'll tell you if he wants you to know. So please don't ask him about it. I'm telling you about it only because things got . . . scary. I got her up and helped them gather their kindling. Shag and I turned to head back for home. I looked up, and there in the trees, watching, stood Mr. Feagans.

And, Miss Anderson, I'm sure he had been there the whole time.

February 18, 1964

As you know, we are writing our own Greek myth in groups. What a cruel trick of the fates, that I was put in a group without Laura Westover this time, but in with Ovita and Omera Stark and David Warren. Neither of the Stark girls says boo in front of other kids, remember, so David and I had to create a play where he and I said all the lines. We quickly realized we were going to have to ask to join with another group, and make Ovita and Omera into dryads, since who expects a tree nymph to talk, right? And whose group wanted to work together? Laura Westover, Frank Charles, and Mildred. Oh, well. Laura took over immediately, but at least she could see the wisdom of Ovita and Omera being dryads.

She also agreed that David should stay Apollo.

"You have a classic body for the god of war," she said. Poor David, he blushed like crazy. "And our only other alternative would be Frank Charles here, and he is the skinniest boy in Bedford County, so you'll have to do." Frank Charles huffed and puffed, but he couldn't deny it, so we moved on.

Today it was nice that the Starks dressed alike. They don't do that most days, as you know. They used to do it all the time—Mr. Stark, Omera and Ovita's daddy, is right proud that he has twin daughters and he wants everybody to know it. He figures when they are dressed alike you can tell from far away that those girls are twins—you don't have to wait to get close enough to see their faces are look-alike images. But Mrs. Warren told him last year that she felt like Ovita and Omera needed to find their own identities, that they were "entirely too wrapped up in each other," and dressing them alike was the first thing that had to go. And like I told you before, when Mrs. Warren says something, snap, people do it. I have to say, the twins are a whole lot more outgoing than they used to be. Just imagine how bad it was before! Come to think on it, as I write in this journal, I see how right Mrs.

Warren was about a lot of things—but don't tell her I said so.

Anyway, Laura looked over the script we'd started. "Not bad," she grudgingly said. "Let's add some scenes with Zeus and Hera—after all, Hera's jealousy is probably going to explain how the dryads got turned into trees—and then we can bring in Aphrodite, the goddess of beauty." She fluffed her blond hair, clearly implying that she would play *that* role. I wanted to throw up.

David said, "Well, I think Kizzy Ann should play that role. She's the prettiest girl here."

Frank Charles punched David in the arm. "You got it sweet for Kizzy Ann, huh?" Frank Charles sort of nodded encouragingly and smiled at David, who blushed furiously and stared at the floor.

Laura erupted. "Kizzy Ann is most certainly *not* the prettiest! She has a big old scar running down her cheek. She can't be Aphrodite! I have to be Aphrodite! Besides, Kizzy Ann is black."

"That's why you can't be Aphrodite," David said. "If I'm Apollo," he explained, pointing to his face, "you can't be Aphrodite. Think about it."

Mildred tried a different approach. "You know, Hera was married to Zeus, and he was the king of the gods. That makes her the queen of the gods. I'm not thinking you want Kizzy Ann to play the queen of anything."

That sure got Laura to shut up. You could see the wheels in her brain spinning. She'd already been planning out what all was going to happen in this play—she had it all mapped out in her mind—and if she took on the role of Aphrodite, she was not going to get to be the queen. It was be the queen or be the prettiest. And if she was the queen, she played opposite the white boy. Things began to fall into place in her mind.

I know you heard some of this, Miss Anderson, but you were stuck with that group that was having a conniption fit about costumes—I guess you were wondering today why you even wanted to be a teacher. Anyway, Mildred did a pretty good job being a peacekeeper, also being the set director. I kept my mouth shut for a change, because I was about *this* close to hauling off and knocking Laura Westover into next week. If she said anything else about my scar, I would have done it, I think.

I don't know how I feel about David Warren and all of this — I was mostly so ticked off at Laura Westover running things I was seeing red, I'll tell you. But I can't believe that old David Warren. And when we were practicing with Shag today, that ridiculous Frank Charles would *not* let it drop. It was David Warren this and David Warren that. Peesh! You'd think a skinny white boy would be a little more careful around a girl who has a dog who will do anything she tells her to. . . .

February 21, 1964

I've thrown away the makeup. I did try it once. I felt I had to do that, after Mr. McKenna spent all that money. I went down to the pond, where I could see it on me. Our pond is just a cow pond, but it is the best place to look on my face in privacy — I told you Granny Bits says having a full-size mirror is pure vanity, and besides, I couldn't let anybody in the house catch me examining my face, touching my scar, sliding my fingers down that stretch of puckered skin. So, to the pond I went. And the pond is a flat of shimmer much of the time, a wide-open reflection. None of our cows were down there today when Shag and I went. I knelt in the dry, wheaty-colored grass and listened to it crackle as I eased my way over to the edge and leaned over to peer at my reflection. I saw myself as I am. Then I closed my eyes, thought of the diagrams I'd seen in the books from the library, and spread the makeup carefully. It did cover the scar some. It made me look different, strange. Shag came and sniffed me. Then she backed up and sat and stared. She lay down and looked at me. I looked again into the pond at myself, at my reflection, and I felt so odd, Miss Anderson. Who was that girl reflecting in the water? It was like she was a whole other person. The makeup didn't bring back the old me. It wasn't the old Kizzy Ann. It was just some other girl, someone I didn't know. It was a disguise, just a disguise.

I don't know as I see the point of it all. I think I would get just as many stares.

I've been thinking a lot on Miss Anne Spencer's

words, about her friend and her cousin, their approaches to life and the layers in between. Remembering how I'd wanted to pull back into myself, cocooned into my corner of bed, but Shag kept facing me out to see the visitors Mama and Daddy brought to my room. Thinking on the fact that my church, my school, and this part of Bedford County rallied to make sure I had company every day for Scrabble games, read-alouds, storytellings by the bedside, and old maid challenges. I didn't have one day when somebody wasn't at my side forcing me to look out at them, forcing them to look back at me. So I think I know how the friend felt: I'm just lucky that I'm surrounded by friends amid the starers. I may change my mind, but for now I feel free and sure. I am like Miss Anne Spencer's friend who had a lot of living to do. I'm not exactly celebrating that people are staring at me, but I'm not going to be ashamed of them looking either. Let them look. I'm a girl with a scar. I'm Moon Child, me, just a girl who can teach her dog some things, while that dog teaches things back.

March 2, 1964

The big spelling bee! I'm a pretty good speller. I've been working all year, and all those reference books I've been reading at your school—I mean our school—must be a help with this, right? They're filled with words that are all in my head now—words I use in this journal, words I use in my head every day when I talk to Sassy and Shag and myself. Winner for the school goes to the state championship in Richmond. Well, that sounds like fun! I've never been to Richmond. I'm starting to study extra hard right now. And now that I'm not worrying about makeup, I've got some space in my head I can fill up with more spelling words. All those words like *countenance* I learned from Miss Anne Spencer could come in handy, right? I'm practicing words too. You didn't even have to give us that pep talk today. I'm going over the dictionary and the Bible. The Bible has lots of beautiful words in it, Miss Anderson. I love words. They just pour over you like hot syrup on corn bread. Drizzle, drizzle, drizzle, rush, rush, rush. I hear you say them all day, I hear them all night in my head

— *153*

when I sleep. I see them behind my eyelids when I practice in class—it's like I just can't miss. I know I'm on my way to Richmond, Miss Anderson. The syrup, the words, are a rush, pouring over me in my mind.

Wouldn't Mrs. Warren have her socks knocked off?

March 5, 1964

I guess you read the paper and you saw that letter to the editor. I almost missed it. I've been working with Mr. McKenna, Frank Charles, and Shag just about every afternoon until dark, and then I help with a few chores and get my homework done. Still, many nights we also go to see James and the JV basketball team. They've been undefeated, just like the JV football, and the local paper just will not put anything in it about them, just like the JV football. It's a stand against integration. Rumor here is that the editor said, "Might can make the schools accept 'em. Can't make me write about 'em."

And then that letter—saying how black or white,

purple or green, athletes should be noted when they're local talent. And that the businesses owned by the signers of the letter would remove their advertising if things didn't get reported on *all* the local athletic teams. . . . And all those signatures, black business-men and white businessmen. Almost one hundred sig-natures. I think Pastor Moore had a hand in it—shoot, I believe he pulled it all together—but it is downright amazing all the same.

Between that and the undefeated season, I'm see-ing my brother return to himself. He works hard for school again, works hard for the farm, and talks to all of us. He and Cabbie are still close, but thank goodness they stopped hanging around with that Montgomery Watkins. He got arrested for breaking into houses last week. Stole from at least twenty people, by the looks of the stuff they found at his house. That could have been James, you know. It could have been us crying like Montgomery's mama did when they took him away in handcuffs.

March 12, 1964

There's a dog trial coming. I can't believe it—Shag may actually have a chance to show off what she knows! It was Frank Charles who brought us the news.

"Holy cow!" he cried. "Did y'all see the bulletin out at the stockyard down on Main Street? A real dog trial, with a judge from Scotland. Any herding dog is allowed to enter. I bet Shag could beat 'em all." He was bouncing, he was so excited.

I looked at Mr. McKenna. "Could she? Is she ready?"

"Better question is, are *you* ready?"

I felt my shoulders sinking.

He shook his head. "Relax, girlie. You are. Depending on the competition you face, you may even place. I don't think you'll win, but perhaps. Not many around here use herding signals from Scotland, as you've been trained. That might help. You may do quite well."

I couldn't sleep last night, Miss Anderson. I'm saying commands in my head, working Shag this way and that in my dreams. Could it really happen?

156 —

I won the bee! The words pouring over my mind, spilling off my tongue! I'm going to Richmond! The rush of beautiful words. I was not amazed at the hug from you—I know by now that you really do love me even if you are white and I am not—but when the crowd gasped, I thought we were in trouble. I think Mrs. Warren saved the day when she came up and wrapped you and me both in a hug that stunned us all. I have never thought I would be so grateful to her. Granny Bits says I will have to write her a thank-you note for all she has done for me. I will, Miss Anderson, I will write, but more than that, I plan to deliver it in person and thank her face-to-face. It is what she deserves, to know that she made this possible for me, by giving up her place as a teacher and giving up the black school so we could come to the white school. Black students have never participated in this spelling bee before. Her stepping aside has made many things possible. It cost her so much, and I don't want her to think I didn't notice.

Of course, I don't know if you have always had a spelling bee for your students, but I am mighty appreciative to you too. Somehow it is even harder to thank you when I know you have to sneak by what you do for all of us or fight for it. I feel as if we have become a burden to you. But you seem to look at all of us the same. I've never seen a white person do that before.

So while Mrs. Warren opened that door, you stepped up to keep it wide. Please don't think we didn't see that too.

We saw, and we see it still.

March 14, 1964

Integrity is the question. The rules don't even say anything about black handlers. It's just assumed that none will be allowed. Frank Charles insists that's my "way in." I know better. Mr. McKenna and Frank Charles came up with an idea—that if Mr. McKenna goes to register with Frank Charles beside him, he could just write the name Kizzy Stamps as handler, and since people down in Lynchburg don't know people from Bedford all that well (especially kids, black or white), he might get away with it. They would just assume

Frank Charles is named Kizzy. Mr. McKenna says once you're registered, you're allowed to compete. I'd surely like to compete.

But.

I've already had Frank Charles lie for me once. And it *was* a lie, even if it was because he kept silent.

I just don't think I can do it. I *won't* do that. It isn't like it was with James. He'd have been in such trouble I can't even imagine. Lying, or letting Frank Charles lie, kept James from being hurt. But this is lying for gain. For Shag to compete, for me to show off what I've learned.

Mr. McKenna and Frank Charles would get in trouble. It wouldn't be like what James would have faced, but there *would* be trouble, mark my words.

And even for Shag, even for me . . . I cannot risk that for my friends.

March 17, 1964

No, ma'am, there's nothing you can do. I just don't see much point in anything right now. I'm not going to

Mr. McKenna's place, not talking with Frank Charles. It isn't to be mean. It isn't to be getting back at anyone. It's just giving up.

March 19, 1964

Mr. McKenna came to my house today. *In* my house today. I'd finished bringing in the cows with Shag, and we were toasting our feet by the fire—it may be toward the end of March, but there's still a big bite in the wind, especially around milking time. There was a beating on the door, and Granny Bits moved to answer. The door burst open before she reached it, though. Burst open, and in marched Mr. McKenna. I knew he was big, and Granny Bits is small (she is named Bits because she's no bigger than two bits), but seeing them close like that was like seeing a giant with an elf.

"Mind your manners," she barked, and he took his hat in his hand.

"Beggin' yer pardon, madam," he said.

"T'ain't no madam. Wipe your feet."

He went back outside, wiped his feet, and asked, "May I see yon lassie by the fire?"

Granny Bits turned to look me over and then smiled. "It's about time someone took her in hand," she said. "Yep, you're welcome to her."

I waited for his bluster, big as the wind blowing in the door. But he closed the door with a quiet chink and just stood before me. His voice came quiet and easy, wrapping around me in ways I was defenseless to fight. "It's no good, girl. It's no good giving in to the fight, no good giving up to the pressure."

What I said sounds hard, now, even to my ears, Miss Anderson, but I meant no disrespect. It was just what was in my heart. "How would you know? How would you know how much I can take, of the back doors and the secondhand clothes, of the 'yes, ma'aming' and 'no, sirring' to people who make no secret they believe they are better than me? How would you know?"

"Alone in the suffering, are you? I come here, to a strange land, to make a living, to seek a dream of owning a herd of sheep of my own. I have the sheep, mind you, I have the living. But the friends I have count as one black poet who warms to the world around her, two children, and a dog. I do not fit in yet, in this country, Kizzy Ann. I don't have to slink in back doors, true, but I am not welcome in the front ones, either.

"But I will not let it stop me. I will not let it beat me.

"And one of the reasons I worked with you and your Shag is because I believed you never would let life beat you either." He knelt then, in front of me, and I had to look him in the eyes, his deep-blue eyes, fringed by those wild and woolly eyebrows. He put out a hand to cradle Shag's jaw, and she closed her eyes as she rested her head in his palm. "She looks to you, girlie, looks to you because you are her world. You've worked hard to earn that love and trust, and I'd hate to see either of you stop before you've won. You're my friends."

"I'll stand there and try to put my name down, and they'll turn me away. In front of everybody," I said. And I couldn't help it, Miss Anderson, I could feel my bottom lip trembling. I don't mind that I did it in front of him, but I would die if I did it in front of all those men at the dog trial. And I know I would. It means that much to me.

He leaned in close to me. "I cannot make it matter less to you, girlie, for it matters a great deal to me as well. All I can promise is that I'll be there with you. And Frank Charles has promised to be there with you too. We'll stand with you. And you know Shag will. It's what you must do, then." He traced my scar and smiled. "You must try, Kizzy Ann, master of this dog at your feet. You must try."

And then Granny Bits asked him to eat with us.

And he did.

March 20, 1964

The strangest thing happened today, Miss Anderson. Shag and I were walking home, and Frank Charles was pretending to be a sheep that wouldn't stay in the path. (This isn't the strange thing it sounds—he does this every so often if Mr. McKenna can't work with us.) Shag will tolerate herding him back to me, although she nips him in tighter tucks than she does the sheep—I think she knows he is playing dumb and that, in Mr. McKenna's words, "the sheep really ken no better." At one point, though, Frank Charles stopped dead and Shag ran right into him. This is not good for my dog—I lit into him.

"You idiot!" I smacked Frank Charles on the arm, knocking him off balance. I looked Shag over, but she was fine. So then I began to help him up. He pulled away and said, "I'm fine. Don't help me, I'm fine." He pointed with his head. "Just watching." I looked up where his head aimed, and there was Mr. Feagans, lurking in the trees. I froze.

I thought I was in for a beating for sure, Miss Anderson, but he just stood there, watching, never moving, watching.

Frank Charles shrugged at me, his voice low. "I can't figure it out. I noticed him there last week," he said. "Thought I was crazy at first, that it must be somebody else, since he didn't charge at us, but no, it was him. He mentioned it at supper, brought it up all easy like . . . 'Saw you walking home from school with the neighbor girl and her dog.'"

I thought my swallow wouldn't make it down my throat. I looked up there again, but he was gone. I looked around, but he didn't seem to be on us, and I looked to Shag. She didn't seem alert to danger, just sniffed at some mushrooms and started to nibble. I cleared a whisper to ask, "Then what did he say?"

"Well, I kept looking at my plate, thought about lying about us, but I remembered how you like the truth and all, so I said 'Yes, sir,' and he didn't say nothing else, Kizzy. That was it." Frank Charles scratched his head. "And then last night he told my mom how your brother came over and helped him with the smoking shed, and he supposed that was kind of decent for a darky, since it was me what messed it up. I almost choked to death on my ham, I tell you."

I looked at Shag, chewing on mushrooms, and then I started walking. "Frank Charles, I don't want to be hurting your feelings or anything, but I don't trust your daddy. That sounds nice and all, but he is still the man who had me beat."

Frank Charles smiled. "Oh, that's okay. I don't trust him either. Not exactly." He shrugged. "He still doesn't like to have your daddy's land next to his land. He's still the same daddy I have always had. I know that. You know that. But he didn't yell just now when he saw me walking with you. His face is probably forty shades of red walking to our house. His gizzard is probably about to pop out of his insides. He's seeing things he has never seen before, but . . . it's like he's trying to get used to them, I guess. He's not liking it, just having to get used to it. He's still my daddy— he ain't happy about all this. Uh-uh. Not happy. But he didn't yell when he saw me walking with you. Or talking to you."

I signaled to Shag to join me. "Yeah. He didn't yell. There is that. Still, I'm keeping both eyes open."

March 21, 1964

Yes, ma'am, I see. I should have known that winning the spelling bee wouldn't have meant I could really go. Of course they wouldn't have a way to reserve a room for a black girl in the hotel. Of course that will mean the runner-up, Laura Westover, will have to go. Of course I understand. You owe me no apology. This is the way things are. This is the way things are for me. I guess Mrs. Warren stepped aside for no good reason.

March 22, 1964

I was down at my pond today, throwing a stick for Shag. Of course who should show up but Frank Charles?

"Thought you said chasing sticks was beneath her," he said.

"It is."

"But you're having her chase a stick."

"Yep."

He stood there watching me continue to throw the stick.

"But you said—"

"Oh, for Pete's sake, Frank Charles, sometimes you are dumber than dirt," I snapped. "I am stuck and frustrated and confused and I'm doing this because I don't know what else to do, you nitwit. I'm mad and disappointed about that stupid spelling bee and I'm confused about the dog trial and I'm still mad you've never apologized about putting a scar on my face and I'm tired of Laura Westover and if you tease me about David Warren liking me again, I will personally knock your smile into space."

"Oh."

I got up and walked toward my house. Shag followed me. I heard footfalls in the grass and felt Frank Charles's hand on my shoulder.

"Kizzy Ann . . . I am so sorry. If I ever could fix anything wrong I've ever done, it would be that, really. I would fix that. I don't think it matters. You're still smart and clever with Shag. And the best speller ever. And you're my friend."

I'm going to try at the dog trial.

March 28, 1964

We walked up from Mr. McKenna's truck, the five of us. Shag, Frank Charles, and I rode in the back, cold though it was. James and Mr. McKenna rode in the cab. James worried that it was a mistake for him to be in the front seat with Mr. McKenna when Frank Charles was in the back, but Mr. McKenna insisted.

"The world can't change unless we start making it change," he said. He patted the front seat at my brother and just kept patting until James joined him. It was Mr. McKenna's truck and his decision. Frank Charles talked on and on about who knows what. I had enough to worry about with the dog trial. My mama had made her famous half-dollar pancakes in my honor, and I hadn't been able to eat a one of them. My stomach was doing so many flips, I just knew I would lose any single solitary bite I put in there.

I led the way to the sign-up table, Shag as close as if she were a part of me. Mr. McKenna was behind with Frank Charles and then James trailing. I was surprised that morning when my brother put on his soft felt hat to join us. He'd shrugged and said, "It seems the right thing to do," and I was taken back to the time I told him about Frank Charles taking the blame for him and those cows crashing down on the smoking shed.

Mist was still clinging to the ground when we'd pulled in at Frank Charles's farm to pick him up. His mother stood at the door when he left to get in the truck with me. She didn't stop him, nor did she wave or say anything to him. I don't know what she thought about him jumping in to sit with a black girl or joining the Scottish man. She simply turned around and let him make his choice. His father wasn't about. Frank Charles nodded to me as he settled in, as close to Shag as she allowed him to move. He put his hands beside her warm body and almost purred. It's times like that when I know for sure why I like him.

Apparently most registration happens on the day of the trial. There was a line to wait in, and Mr. McKenna, Shag, and I stood our turn while Frank Charles and James lurked off to the side. There were the smells of men — Old Spice mixed with perspiration, mingled with chewing tobacco. In the low murmur of voices, not a single woman's voice was in the mix. Not a welcoming place for a girl. And of course, no blacks. The cool breeze touching my neck and dancing across my face couldn't ease the nervous energy that felt like fire burning out of me. Perhaps it didn't show, but I felt like I was a ball of flame ready to explode. Finally I stepped to the front, reached for the pencil to enter my name, and put down my two-dollar fee. As expected, a hand blocked mine. "No."

I kept my eyes down. Shag tensed. I put my hand on her back. I heard a low growl beginning and could feel it pulsing under her fur.

Mr. McKenna spoke. "I'm sponsoring the girl," he said.

Someone said, "We don't want trouble."

Again Mr. McKenna spoke. "I agree, no trouble. We just want to compete. Fair and square. The girl and her dog."

Another voice: "No darkies."

Mr. McKenna said, "This is a time of integration."

"Law says schools—nothing says anything about anywhere else."

I looked up and around—all of these voices coming from faces I couldn't really see, Miss Anderson, no one speaking out in the open, no one brave enough to actually stand in the light and say these words. I started to shake, and I could feel myself wanting to give up, to give in, to go home. I could also feel myself getting angry, getting steely, getting ready to say something that might get me another switching like the one I had at the command of Mr. Feagans. I was afraid that ball of flame inside me really would explode and burn up everyone around me, including Shag. I didn't want that. Where was something to steady me?

My bottom lip trembled, and you know I didn't

want that either. Crying never helps. I took a deep breath and put my hand down to reach for my Shag. Then, of course, my words came out simple and strong: "I can't talk as pretty as poets. I don't know what to say to make things right.

"But I can handle my dog. I can handle these sheep. My dog is good. All we want is a chance to show you. We want to try."

James stepped up beside me on one side. Frank Charles stepped up on the other.

Mr. Feagans stepped out of nowhere from the crowd. He pointed to the judge from Scotland with his head and said to him, "You okay with a black girl competing?"

The old man, red haired, wrinkled, and clutching a walking stick, looked at me briefly and then focused on Shag. He looked her over carefully, took a step back, and looked her over again. "Dog looks good. Girl only matters if she can handle the dog."

Mr. Feagans looked at Frank Charles, then back at me, and took a deep breath. He shrugged once to the others. "Not like it really hurts things, does it?" He looked around. "Not like she'll win," he said. He laughed nervously. The others backed away then. He looked at me, nodded once, then moved off quickly.

I was frozen, but Mr. McKenna punched me in the shoulder and said in a very quiet voice, "Move, girl, before he changes his mind." I grabbed the pencil so quickly I almost dropped it, wrote my name as fast as ever I could, and just like that, we had our chance. Mr. McKenna moved me away from the bundle of men in a hurry. Off to the side, he scooped me into a hug that left me breathless. Frank Charles grabbed Shag into a sort of hug that left her growling at him, and James just scratched his head. We were twenty-first in the mix, and we moved away to watch the dogs ahead of us.

Miss Anderson, I still can't believe I had my chance. I felt I had to memorize everything then, had to take in every memory because I might never have this again. I'm not stupid. There may be rules to stop me if I try to come again.

The competition was at Lonnie McLean's New London farm. The meadow was lush and green. The day was crisp but not cold—one of those righteous first days of spring. I didn't pay any attention to his farmhouse—that was of no interest. The place we would be working the sheep was wide and just right for Shag and the other dogs. I could see Mr. McKenna nodding as he took it all in.

The judge ran the show like Mrs. Warren used to run her math quizzes: no-nonsense and fast. He called the first handler, who came out with his dog at ten fourteen, and things moved like clockwork from that point on. A farmer I've never seen from Campbell County went in that first slot. He had a shaggy sheepdog—a rolling stack of hair and bark. They did well, although the dog didn't pen the sheep quickly.

"You could have beat that," Frank Charles said to Shag. He makes most of his positive comments to her, but I know he means me too.

"Perhaps," Mr. McKenna said.

I didn't say anything. I didn't know what to say. Still, Frank Charles was right: Shag is lots faster than that dog was.

The next two contestants, both with collies, did well also. I saw where the handlers were better than me, crisper in their commands, surer in their decisions, but neither dog could touch Shag.

They all began to blur into each other as I started to gain more and more of my vision of how I would run Shag, how I would get those sheep to the pen. I remembered all the times I'd drawn Mr. McKenna's wrath, all the times I'd depended on Shag to save me, and I knew I couldn't let my dog down so badly again. I watched and tried to think. I admit, Miss Anderson, my nerves were getting the best of me.

And suddenly it was our turn. I moved to the handler's stake and sent Shag in her outrun. She went, and when I didn't see her, I got nervous. I started with as many points as I could get—I'd lose points for every mistake, but fewer points if I redirected her than if she kept making mistakes, so I shouted, "Get back!" I saw her then and realized she was right where she was supposed to be. I'd cost us points because I hadn't trusted her. The sheep kept coming. I flanked Shag at the wrong time. She cut an eye at me (she knew *I'd* been wrong), but she followed my command and I saw more points flying away. I gathered myself, gave better commands, and she kept those sheep moving. She was quick and efficient, and she got them circling to the pen. We'd lose points if they circled *around* the pen, and Shag sensed this, so without my command, she maneuvered them so they were penned and in the gates. We finished with a satisfactory number of our points intact, thanks to my dog and at least a little of the training Mr. McKenna put into me.

More contestants came after me, but my head was spinning as I put my dog in the tub of ice water to cool her down after the tiring, hot experience. I sloshed water over her neck and back and pulled the cooling water through her fur as I caressed her. "We did it, girl. You did it, girl," I said. I looked to my friends, my friends who were there for me, there *with* me, this finest moment of my life. I knew that it didn't matter whether we won any place at all. For that experience, on that course, I was an equal.

Miss Anderson, we won third place! When he handed me the ribbon, the judge said, "That is one special dog, miss." He shook my hand, then added, "You're not so bad yourself, but ye've got to learn to trust."

I looked at him. "I'm working on that one. Yes, sir."

And after that, lots of people came up to look at Shag, people I didn't know. I watched folks I didn't know touch my dog, and I watched Shag, allowing hands to touch her, allowing herself to risk so much. And how can I do less than my dog, even if that dog is my incredible, incredible Shag?

How can I do less than believe and hope and fight and try?

May 6, 1964

I went to see Mrs. Warren today, to thank her for all she did for the black people of this county. She did not make it easy for me, Miss Anderson. You might think the old biddy would have been gracious when someone took the time to come and say thank you, but no, she received me in her living room like some queen in England. She had David show me in.

"David says you wish to speak with me about something, Kizzy Ann."

She was sitting in her best chair, a striped Queen Anne that has seen better days, frankly, as it is faded and frumpy and the bottom has no springs left in it because she sits in it every day and she is a large lady, shall we say. I don't mean to be ugly, just honest. And honestly, she was just being so highfalutin it was ridiculous. I know David had told her what I was coming for.

I said, "I wanted to thank you for giving up your place at the black school so we could all go study at the white school and all. They have reference books, and it really has been the opportunity you said it would be, and we even had a spelling bee, even if we didn't get to go to Richmond because no black student could win."

That broke her lordy act. She looked at me and sighed. "It won't be easy, child. Rome wasn't built in a day." She heaved up out of that chair and went to stand at her window that looks out over her yard. "But give it time, Kizzy Ann. You won the bee, David said." She looked at me and smiled. "They know around here that you're smart, and I always knew you could do it."

Then she snapped her eyes at me. "And it's about time somebody thanked me for all I done." She yelled down the hall, "David, bring that iced tea and pound cake in here!" She gave me a smile.

The end-of-school ceremony was fine, Miss Anderson. The punch with orange sherbet floating in it was so good. The homemade three-layer cake was scrumptious. I know you wanted people to mingle better, to see a mix of white and black instead of all the white people on one side and the blacks on the other. But give it time, Miss Anderson. Give it time.

I wore the white dress again, for Mama and for you. And I talked to Laura Westover for almost five minutes. She was trying as hard as I was, you know. She told me she knew I should have been there in Richmond, and that she believed I would have won the whole contest. Maybe. Who knows? And I don't think she peeked at my scar once. She really just looked into my eyes. Five minutes. I never thought I'd see it.

Winning that certificate for my writing was a perfect finish to a hard year. I never expected that, but Mama and Daddy were so proud. Granny Bits says we will hang it right over that sliver of mirror, so that every time anyone checks his or her face, it's right there to see how good a writer I am.

James gave me a present, for the end of the school year. It's a journal, and I figure you helped him get a hold of it. Embossed in the leather, right where my fingers can find it whenever I want, are the words *Moon Child*. Mama cried at that. And I did just a little. I thank you. It is beautiful, and the pages are creamy and just waiting for me to fill them with my adventures with Shag and Frank Charles and Mr. McKenna. And maybe a few with David Warren. Mama still thinks I might write poetry like Miss Anne Spencer. And I'm thinking I might spend a little more time with Miss Anne—a lady like her can teach somebody like me a whole lot.

James said, "It's for you to write your story. Fill it with words, powerful words. And Mrs. Warren says you'll be a leader one day!"

I don't know about leading, Miss Anderson. I'm headstrong, for sure, and I love to learn new things. But I've seen on my pages to you how many times I give up and give in. The difference for me is Shag . . . wanting to help her and wanting to do right by her. I think she leads me. She and I are both learning a lot about trust—some hard lessons, but true even when they take us far from where we thought we'd be. I promise to follow her, follow to what is right and fair. We've already found some friends who will go with us on the way. We only have to let them join us. That was hard for both of us, for both Shag and I are hard-pressed to ask for help, but we're learning to lean on others. We're learning to trust, we are. The lessons we're learning together along this road are not the easiest, but once we have them, we "own" them, you might say. When I follow my Shag, it seems I follow my heart.

I guess that will do just fine.

July 1, 1964

Dear Kizzy Ann,

Your letter arrived today, and I am so excited
to read of your further adventures with Frank
Charles, Mr. McKenna, and, of course, Shag!
Yes, indeed, you must keep writing to me, and
I will write back.

 I am heartened to hear of plans to turn the
old schoolhouse into a community center—and
I am not surprised to learn that you and Mrs.
Warren will lead the endeavor! This means it
<u>will</u> happen, no matter what. Poor Mr. Felix—
I think he will be custodian forever. . . .

 I know you may not want to hear this, but I
have purchased journals for the new class—and
I can assure you, there is no one, in this year's
class or in any class to come, who will take your
place in my heart. You, and that dog of yours,

182 —

are one in a million (well, two in a million). I
am counting on you, Miss Kizzy Ann Stamps,
to be the student I have taught who grows up to
do really great things. Every teacher hopes she
has touched every student in special ways, but she
has to believe that there is one who is going to go
on to light up the world.

You are my one, Kizzy. I don't know how
you will or when you will. But you have already
done some of that in my life. I just know you can
make a difference. You may be a girl who doesn't
like bows or fancy dresses (both things I like very
much), but what does that matter? You are my
girl, Kizzy Ann. And you are your own person.

Love,
Miss Anderson

AUTHOR'S NOTE

Anne Spencer was, indeed, a real person: a librarian and poet who lived in Lynchburg. She did not, however, have a library in her home, nor did she have a cousin who had an accident as I've described it, nor do I know if she gave advice or had conversations as I've described. These are examples of literary license. You can visit Anne Spencer's real home in Lynchburg and read her poetry to find out more about her. She was an amazing woman, and I hope her living family will feel pleased by how she appears in this book; my intention was to honor her.

The American Kennel Club is represented in this book as not allowing African Americans to participate in the early 1960s, and as far as I could find out, this is accurate. It is also accurate that border collies were not yet an accepted breed in the AKC at that time. None of this should be taken as a negative statement toward this organization as it exists today. The AKC does many wonderful things for the dogs of the world, including border collies, and they also encourage and support dog owners across the country. In the story, Kizzy Ann's view of the organization is informed by what she hears from those around her, and she is, of course, focused on what directly affects her and Shag.

ACKNOWLEDGMENTS

This book was written over many years. Thus I may not remember to thank someone who has been vital to its development, and if that is you, reader, I sincerely apologize. But at the risk of leaving someone out, I want to thank those I do remember.

One of the sparks for this story happened at a teachers' workshop when fellow teacher Sandy Claytor and I were paired up to work on improving a piece of writing. This particular piece was about a dog, and in the process of our work on it, Sandy shared stories about her own dog—named, you guessed it, Shag. Thank you, Sandy, for giving me the heart of Shag.

So many of the students I've worked with over the years—at Waddell Elementary School, the University of Virginia, Lynchburg College, and in classroom visits—have listened to pieces of this book: thank you for helping, in ways you didn't even realize, to shape this story.

Thank you to teachers everywhere, teachers like the one in this book, who make a difference every day for the students who depend on you. Having taught for twenty-seven years in public school, I now prepare teacher candidates to go out in the world, and I am also blessed with many schoolteachers in my family. They are all people who open their hearts every day to children who need them. What an amazing profession. Bravo to every teacher in the world. A tough job performed by tender hearts.

Members of my Lynchburg Community Race Dialogue Study Circle: you contributed to this story in our rich discussions and sharing your own stories.

While I have always loved dogs and my family always had at least one dog in all my years of growing up (and I started life on a farm in Bedford County), we never lived with a border collie. So I thank Amy Yoho, secretary of the Virginia Border Collie Association, who kindly reviewed the manuscript. (But do note that any remaining border-collie-related errors are mine and mine alone!)

I thank Lynchburg College and, in particular, Jan Stennette, dean of the School of Education and Human Development, who allowed me some release time to work on this book. I have never been given professional time for my writing before, and having this gift was amazingly meaningful to me. It is so powerful to work in an atmosphere where my work is appreciated. A dear friend and colleague, Dr. Susan Thompson, professor at Lynchburg College, volunteers to read everything I write and gives me feedback but mostly unconditional acceptance. Thank you, Susan.

The Good Ole Girls writing group in Lexington, Virginia, heard an early draft and liked it. That inspired me to keep writing when I might have just put it aside.

My very bestest friend, Gay Lynn Van Vleck, who is an incredible writer, has been a support to me for so many years. Thank you for believing in me some years when I didn't believe in myself. And her family, Bill and Jack, are as dear as the day is long!

Thanks to very helpful readers Dr. Loretta Jones, Deidre Washington, and Ginny Shank.

To all the readers, editors, helpers, and friendly voices at Candlewick Press—Kate Fletcher, Hilary Van Dusen, Andrea Tompa, Carter Hasegawa, Nikki Bruno Clapper, Hannah Mahoney and, of course, my first and most important editor, the incomparable Liz Bicknell—where would I be without all of you? I wish I could wrap you all in a hug. Thank you, thank you, for bringing my Kizzy Ann to the page with spunk and fire and for giving her and Shag a home at Candlewick, the best publisher in the world!

I'd also like to thank the James River Writers Organization; it was at their annual conference where I was able to make contact with Candlewick, and I am most grateful.

And finally, and most important, I thank my family. The family I grew up in, the family that surrounded me as I wrote this book, and the family that grew away from me, spreading out in their own places in the world—all of them very kindly believing in me still and supporting me in their own way. I needed them, and they answered, maybe without even knowing. So, to Chandler and Daryl; Mary Carson and Gavin; Jill, Greg, Gretchen, and Katie—I thank you for support you may never have known you gave. And Chuck . . . well, you always knew. And I thank you now and forever.